W9-CHR-002

"Those guys mean nothing to me," Lori said.

"Well, I was beginning to wonder," Andy said, *"what with your making up to Sammy like that and kissing Joe—"*

"Kissing Joe!" Lori said indignantly. *"If you only knew how awful that was!"* She made a face and added, *"I've pretty much decided that I'm not the romantic type!"*

"Seems like you had the wrong partner," Andy said, his eyes twinkling. He drew Lori toward him and kissed her firmly on the mouth.

Her lips curved happily beneath his sweet, warm pressure. Should she admit that he was absolutely, one hundred percent right?

Dear Reader,

At Silhouette we publish books with you in mind. We're pleased to announce the creation of Silhouette First Love, a new line of contemporary romances written by the finest young-adult writers as well as outstanding new authors in this field.

Silhouette First Love captures many of the same elements enjoyed by Silhouette Romance readers—love stories, happy endings and the same attention to detail and description. But First Love features young heroines and heroes in contemporary and recognizable situations.

You play an important part in our future plans for First Love. We welcome any suggestions or comments on our books and I invite you to write to us at the address below.

Karen Solem
Editor-in-Chief
Silhouette Books
P.O. Box 769
New York, N.Y. 10019

FOR
THE LOVE
OF LORI
Veronica Ladd

First Love from Silhouette

Published by Silhouette Books New York

America's Publisher of Contemporary Romance

Other First Loves by Veronica Ladd

Flowers for Lisa
Promised Kiss

SILHOUETTE BOOKS, a Simon & Schuster Division of
GULF & WESTERN CORPORATION
1230 Avenue of the Americas, New York, N.Y. 10020

Copyright © 1982 by Veronica Ladd

Distributed by Pocket Books

All rights reserved, including the right to reproduce
this book or portions thereof in any form whatsoever.
For information address Silhouette Books, 1230
Avenue of the Americas, New York, N.Y. 10020

ISBN: 0-671-53329-0

First Silhouette Books printing October, 1982

10 9 8 7 6 5 4 3 2 1

All of the characters in this book are fictitious. Any resem-
blance to actual persons, living or dead, is purely coincidental.

SILHOUETTE, FIRST LOVE FROM SILHOUETTE
and colophon are trademarks of Simon & Schuster.

America's Publisher of Contemporary Romance

Printed in the U.S.A.

With love and gratitude,
For my sister, Anne Seislove,
Who took the other path
In Our Enchanted Orange Grove

There was a strange man

1

Lori Valentino was whistling as she pedaled down the street toward Andy's house. The sun was shining so brightly that the gray Cape Cod houses seemed silver against the bright blue sky. It was going to be a good day, Lori thought, and she tried a few bird imitations, just for the fun of it.

The bird imitations were her best friend Andy's specialty, not hers. He'd always been able to whistle better than she could, but she never gave up trying. One of these days, she would get a sound that could pass for a robin. Or at least a blue jay, Lori thought, and she laughed aloud as she pictured herself calling Andy up and whistling the loud, angry call of a blue jay over the telephone.

There was a strange car in Andy's

driveway. Lori hoped that whoever it was wouldn't hold up their fishing trip. On a day like this, fishing was the most important thing in the world. She hopped off the bike and pushed it up the gravel driveway past the blue Cadillac. Who would be driving a big car like that these days? It didn't seem as though any of Andy's parents' friends would dare park such a gas guzzler in the Johnson front yard. The Johnsons owned a health food store and were strong believers in the conservation of energy. So were all their friends, as far as Lori knew—and she certainly knew plenty about the Johnsons. She and Andy had been best friends for eleven years now. Ever since kindergarten, she'd been running in and out of the Johnson house as though it were her own.

Part of the reason they'd been able to remain such good friends was the kind of parents that Andy had. They wanted their son to grow up with modern attitudes toward women. Their understanding had helped Andy and Lori through some rough years in junior high school, when, one by one, they'd watched the boys and girls separate themselves from friendships with each other and start dating. Even when Andy started dating, their friendship hadn't changed. Lori had the feeling that it might be more complicated when she started dating, but she was sure they'd manage.

But whose car was it? Maybe it's one of Tim's friends, Lori thought. Tim was Andy's older brother, who lived in an apartment on the other side of Eastham. Of all the Johnsons, he was the one who was most likely to have a friend with a car like that. Tim was a computer engineer and not much like his folks at all. His politics were conservative, and he preferred steak to sprouts; in hundreds of other ways, he seemed more old-fashioned than his parents.

Lori knocked lightly on the front door and opened it, calling at the same time, "Andy? Are you ready?"

"Come on in," Andy called. Lori could tell by his voice that he wasn't ready to go fishing. She stepped inside the entryway of the house and walked toward the living room. Andy must be talking to the guests. She hoped they wouldn't have to hang around too long.

Lori's guess had been right. Tim was sitting stiffly on the wide green velvet hassock in front of the fireplace. Even though it was Saturday, he was dressed in a sports jacket and tie. Beside him sat a young blond woman.

Andy stood up and said, "Lori, this is Patricia Patterson. And her mother and father. You know her cousin Melissa."

Lori nodded to Melissa, who didn't seem to see her. She knew Melissa all right, but Melissa didn't always recognize her, even though they'd been in the same schools since third grade. They could never be friends, Lori knew, but it seemed silly that Melissa often ignored her. Melissa always saw Andy and other boys, Lori noted. So there was nothing wrong with her eyes.

Mr. and Mrs. Patterson sat on the edge of the old corduroy sofa. They were all dressed up; he wore a navy suit, and she had on a print dress and high-heeled shoes. Lori thought they looked out of place and uncomfortable in the Johnson living room.

Patricia Patterson was pretty, and her blond hair curled around her face the same way Melissa's did. Mrs. Patterson, Patricia, and Melissa all looked alike. What are they doing here? Lori wondered.

"Tim's getting married," Andy's mother said. She was sitting on a low rattan stool in one corner of the room. Lori thought she looked unhappy about her announcement, even though she was smiling as she said it.

"That's nice," Lori said. She turned to look at Andy with an unspoken question. But Andy wasn't looking at her. His head was turned, and he was looking at Melissa Gaylord as though he'd never seen her before. That was silly because Andy had also known Melissa since the third grade. Not that they'd ever been friends. I have friends who are boys, Lori thought, and she has boyfriends.

For the first time, the thought that Andy might be interested in some other girl seemed painful to Lori. She wished she hadn't come here today. She didn't like looking at the way Andy was looking at Melissa. Of course, it had nothing to do with her, but it still made her uncomfortable.

Why would he be interested in a girl like that? Melissa was like a big, fluffy ball of cotton candy. No substance.

She could tell Andy's mother, Ruth Johnson, agreed because she said rather sharply, "Run along, Andy, if you want to."

Mrs. Johnson would agree with her about Melissa, Lori knew. In fact, Mrs. Johnson and Lori agreed about most things, including the opinion that her oldest son was stuffy and old-fashioned. More than once, she'd heard Mrs. Johnson shake her head and say, "We changed too much, too late." Then, she'd been a school teacher, and Mr. Johnson had been a banker. For them to be the parents of Tim wasn't so surprising. But then the Johnsons had quit their jobs, opened the health food store, gotten active in yoga, anti-nuclear politics and environmental action committees. Tim hadn't followed in their path. Tim went right on being the way he'd always been, and that was sad, Lori thought.

But none of that was any of her business, she knew.

Anyway, it was too beautiful a day to worry. "Let's go," she said to Andy.

"But you haven't said you'd do it," Melissa said. She put her hand on

12

Andy's arm and smiled up at him with her blue eyes batting fast and furiously.

"He doesn't want to," Ruth Johnson said. She turned to her elder son and said, "If you want a formal wedding, that's your business. But I'm not going to let you bully Andy into doing something he doesn't want to do."

Patricia's smile was a wider, brighter version of Melissa's. Lori decided she probably wouldn't like her much either. Patricia said, "But I want Melissa to be maid of honor. She *needs* Andy. An older man wouldn't look right."

"Andy's too young," Ruth Johnson protested.

"He's sixteen. Same age as I am," Melissa said.

Lori, who was still standing in the doorway, felt as though she were watching a play. She could almost read the thoughts of every character in the room. There was Tim, looking honest and sober, hoping his mother wouldn't disgrace him in front of his bride-to-be and her proper family.

The bride-to-be and her parents were probably thinking that Tim came from a very peculiar family. Though Mrs.

Johnson was wearing shoes today, her white cotton yoga pants and scarlet leotard were hardly the costume they would expect on the groom's mother. Mr. and Mrs. Patterson were perched so close to the edge of the sofa that Lori thought they might try to fly away.

Patricia's mother dyed her hair a shade darker than her daughter's honey blond, while Ruth Johnson let her gray hair fall loosely around her face. The two women might be close to the same age, but they looked as though they came from such different worlds that it was surprising to hear them talking the same language.

Lori supposed that Tim would be happier with people like the Pattersons for in-laws than he was with his own parents. It was clear that he agreed with them about the wedding. Tim was probably getting the girl and in-laws he needed, Lori thought. He would be all right.

It's Andy who has the problem, Lori thought. Of all the people in the room, Andy seemed to be the one who was looking most unhappy. He was such a soft-hearted person. He would hate to say no to Tim, Lori knew. Poor Andy was caught in the middle, and that silly Melissa wasn't helping.

"You will, won't you?" Melissa demanded. Then she smiled and turned to her mother quickly saying, "That's settled then."

Lori hadn't heard Andy agree to anything, but Patricia and her mother started talking about the colors for the wedding. Ruth Johnson leaned forward, looking as though she wanted to say something, but Andy put his hand on her arm. Lori smiled because the gesture was exactly the same as his father's. Usually his mother did all the talking in the Johnson family and his dad said very little. But he could always calm her down with a word, a hug, or a simple touch. Lori thought they had a wonderful marriage. She wondered if Tim would do as well as his folks.

His mother was leaning back now, with a polite expression on her face. She started stretching her legs forward, pointing one toe at a time. Lori knew she was doing foot exercises while she listened to the conversation.

Finally, the Pattersons got up to leave, seeming pleased with the outcome of the conversation. As Melissa passed her in the doorway, she stopped and said, "Oh Lori. How long have you been here?"

Lori couldn't think of anything to say that wouldn't sound surly, so she shrugged and said, "A while."

"Then you know that Andy and I are going to be in a wedding together." Melissa's smile was a little pink bow. Her eyes seemed to say she was not quite sure she was teasing as she put her hand on Andy's arm again and turned to Lori to ask, "You won't be jealous, will you?"

Lori kept her voice as flat as she could as she answered, "No, should I be?"

Ruth Johnson laughed. Andy looked away, and Melissa pretended she hadn't heard her. When they were all out of the front door, Ruth Johnson hugged Lori and said, "I didn't know how much I loved you until I saw that child. It's a crime what they're doing to that girl!"

Lori didn't answer. She knew that Ruth Johnson would have liked to say a lot more, but Andy said, "Let's get out of here."

Lori followed Andy out of the house and into the garage, where he unlocked his bicycle. Then she asked, "You're not really going to be in that wedding, are you?"

"Why not?"

"Big weddings are silly." She wanted to add that the Pattersons and Melissa were silly people, but she didn't dare. Andy looked up to Tim and was often sensitive when his mother criticized him.

"I don't know what's wrong with my folks," Andy said. "They're so critical of Tim. He wants a big wedding. Why shouldn't he have one?"

"They're expensive and silly. Everyone will be all dressed up and act phony. It would kill me," Lori said.

"Don't worry," Andy said. "No one's going to ask *you* to be best man." He grinned and climbed on his bicycle, balancing the fishing poles across the handlebars. Lori picked up the tackle box and strapped it to the back fender of her bike. Clearly, the discussion about the wedding was over. It wasn't any of her business anyway. If Andy wanted to walk down the aisle with that silly Melissa, that was his decision.

Nevertheless, after they'd settled in on the wharf at the landing and dropped their lines in the water, Lori broached the subject again. She asked, "Did you know Tim was going to get married?"

"I did," Andy said. "Last time he came home from college, he told me. But Mom just found out last night."

"She was upset?"

Andy laughed. "You might say. She tried to keep her cool, but Dad said a few things that really hurt Tim. They had a big row."

"That why your father wasn't there today?"

"Sort of. One of them had to work in the store, and he was still so mad that Mom stayed home."

"Mad because Tim's marrying Patricia?"

"They'd never say that," Andy said. "They only said they were mad about the big wedding. But you know, they're really mad because Tim isn't just like them. Sometimes I think my folks are just as narrow-minded as anyone else's."

Lori thought about the other parents she knew. "No," she said. "Your folks are better. They may be a little opinionated on the subject of food."

"Opinionated!" Andy interrupted. "They think anyone who eats a candy bar is going straight to the hospital with an overdose of sugar."

"But they're better than most kids' parents," Lori assured him. "They're fun, and they listen. They seem young, and they don't try to push you into a mold."

Andy looked out over the blue water as he said, "Yes they do. They try to push you into a mold, just like the Pattersons and the other adults do. Only their mold is health food and energy conservation and yoga and stuff like that."

"It's a better mold," Lori said.

"Better for you," Andy replied. "You like my folks because you happen to agree with them. But they're still narrow-minded."

"So you're going to be in the wedding?" Lori asked, changing the subject. She felt too happy to fight with Andy.

"I haven't decided," Andy admitted. "I feel sorry for Tim. But I don't really want to be in that sideshow."

"Then don't be in it," Lori said. "Tim will understand."

"I hate being in the middle," Andy said gloomily. Seems like Tim and my folks are always trying to make me choose between them. I hate that."

"You're lucky you've got such a nice family," Lori said. She was an only child, and her father had died when she was young, so she really envied Andy's family life. Besides, she liked his parents. In fact, Mrs. Johnson was probably her second best friend. It's not that I don't love my own mother, Lori thought. It's just that Ruth is a very special person.

"You think you'd like living in a big family," Andy said. "But you and your mother have an easy life. It gets complicated when you have to negotiate everything."

Lori laughed out loud. "Tim lives in his own apartment. Your sister is away at college. Your mom and dad and you aren't exactly a big family." It seemed to her that Andy was taking the whole thing too seriously. His folks would get over it if he decided to be best man. And if he didn't, Tim would find someone else. Should she tell him that? Lori glanced sideways at him.

"Melissa wants me," Andy said gloomily.

Lori laughed. "Melissa is such a flirt, she wants any boy."

Andy whipped around and said, "Forget it, will you?"

"Pardon me," Lori said in exaggerated politeness. Then she quickly changed the subject. Obviously, Andy was more upset than she had realized. Was it because of Melissa? Lori was surprised at how the thought troubled her. Why should she care? It was Andy's business, not hers.

2

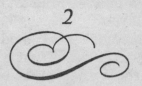

One. Two. Three. Four." Andy Johnson counted under his breath, trying to keep his steps as slow and steady as the music. Being best man at his brother's wedding was just as bad as he'd expected. "Never, never, never," he said under his breath to the accompaniment of the organ music. Even if he decided to get married someday in the far off future, he would elope. Elopement was better. Cheaper. More direct. More honest.

His feet seemed to tangle, and he brought his mind back to the problem at hand—getting up the aisle without stumbling. He reminded himself that he was an athlete, one who was known for his grace on the baseball diamond. Walking down an aisle should be a piece of cake. When they got to the altar, he sighed with relief. Halfway home, he told himself.

"To your left," his brother Tim hissed. Andy quickly moved to his appointed position, hoping no one noticed he was out of step.

The minister was talking, and Andy listened for his cue. First, there was the part about the bond of marriage, and then there were the questions. Andy smiled as he remembered his family's horror at the old-fashioned ceremony. His mother had threatened not to attend the wedding if they left in the bride's promises to love, honor, and "obey" the groom. The bride's mother had finally agreed to the more modern "cherish."

Right after those questions, Andy reminded himself that he was supposed to produce the ring. The ring! His fingers searched his pockets. The ring wasn't there!

He looked out at the church spectators, as though someone out there could tell him where he'd put the ring. His eyes landed on Lori. He wanted to call out to her and ask if she remembered where he'd put the ring. But that was stupid. Lori couldn't help him.

The more his fingers searched, the more certain he was that he would never find the ring. He began to feel along the inside of the pocket seams. Perhaps there was a hole? No.

Melissa Gaylord whispered, "Your vest. Check your vest." Andy's fingers moved up to his vest pocket, where the ring lay waiting.

The minister turned to Andy, saying, "The ring, please."

Andy's hand shot out, and he dropped the ring into Tim's hand. His brother winked at him and kissed his bride.

Andy breathed a sigh of relief and turned to Melissa Gaylord, who smiled brilliantly at him, her white, even teeth sparkling in the light from the stained glass window over the altar. The organist struck up a joyous song. Tim leaned over and kissed Patricia a second time, then the bride and groom linked arms and started down the aisle. Melissa slipped her arm into Andy's and looked at him with bright blue eyes. He was very aware of her light touch on his arm.

Once outside the church, she leaned over and whispered in his ear, "I'm going to catch this bouquet. I just know

I am. Wish me luck, Andy." She smelled of a light flowery perfume, and her lips brushed his earlobe. Andy felt a sharp tingle of pleasure that started in his ear and ran down his spine.

Melissa ran lightly down the stairs. The people were coming out of the church now, walking on either side of the wedding party down to the sidewalk in front of the church. As they walked, they were laughing and smiling. They seemed to Andy to be a blur of faces and voices. He saw some of the cousins from the bride's side of the family. Several people spoke to him by name, but the only face that really registered was Lori's.

Lori walked by him and jabbed his arm. She laughed. "You looked pretty weird up there. I thought for a minute you were going to run out of the church," she said.

Andy grinned at Lori. It didn't surprise him that Lori knew how nervous he was. Being friends for eleven years can teach you a lot about someone.

But he could think about Lori any old day. It was Melissa Gaylord who was on his mind. He watched her as she stood at the bottom of the stairs waiting for

25

the bride to toss the wedding bouquet. What would it be like to kiss a girl like Melissa? She was so small and pretty. It must feel like holding a doll to hold her. And kissing her would be . . .

Melissa lifted her slim arms, reached up on her tiptoes and squealed in delight as the pink and yellow summer flowers came zooming through the air in her direction. "I've got it!" she called. She would have, too, if Lori's longer, browner, more muscular arms hadn't shot out in front of her.

Andy admired Lori's effortless reach. She had the grace of an athlete. He felt sorry for Melissa, who looked almost as though she might cry. Suddenly, Andy felt angry at Lori. What did she need crummy old flowers for anyway? A girl with a potential career as a professional baseball player certainly didn't need to be thinking about catching bridal bouquets. Could it be that Lori had only caught the flowers to annoy Melissa? Then he dismissed that idea. It wasn't like Lori, who didn't have a mean bone in her body. Lori just couldn't resist a good, competitive catch.

Lori was looking down at the flowers as though she were surprised to see them in her hands. He slipped down into the crowd long enough to say to Lori in a teasing voice, "You know what that means, don't you? It means you're going to be the next one to get married."

Lori sniffed. "Here, you want them?" She handed the flowers to Andy.

"What am I supposed to do with them?" he asked.

"I don't care," Lori answered. "I only caught them because it looked so easy."

"I'll give them away." He turned toward Melissa, who was talking to an older couple. Lori walked toward his mother and father.

When Melissa saw Andy, she smiled and slipped her arm through his. Again he felt the same pleasurable reaction as he smelled her flowery perfume and enjoyed the tingle of her touch. She said, "Thank you for rescuing the flowers for me. I don't know what Lori would want them for anyway. She'll probably never get married."

Andy flushed and his spine stiffened as it always did if anyone criticized Lori. Not that anyone criticized their friendship anymore. They had fought that out on grade school playgrounds

27

long ago. He said, "Lori's my friend, you know."

Melissa squeezed his arm and smiled at him as she said, "I know. But even you have to admit that she's a tomboy."

Andy shrugged. "That's an old-fashioned word. I don't think Lori would like to have it used about her."

He tried to hit a middle tone between defending his friend and not making Melissa uncomfortable. He liked having Melissa close to him and liked feeling her hand on his arm. He was enjoying it more than he could have ever guessed.

Andy talked with the older couple for a few minutes, then it was time to get into the cars and drive to the country club for the wedding reception. He looked around for Lori, hoping that he would be able to ride in the same car with her. Usually Lori was easy to find because she was taller than most of the people in the crowd, but he couldn't see her.

Melissa asked, "Don't you think we ought to ride over together?"

Andy nodded his head, and Melissa, still holding onto his arm, led him through the crowd to a Cadillac. They sat in the back seat with a fat aunt of Melissa's. Andy had to put his arm around Melissa to make room, and he enjoyed having her so close to him. Would she go out with him if he asked her? Was she just flirting with him because they were in the wedding party?

Andy kept turning his head to look at the pretty girl with the golden blond hair and the big blue eyes. She moved her hands and arms a lot as she talked, and just about everything she said was punctuated with dainty little laughs.

When they got to the country club, Melissa seemed to expect Andy to stay with her for the rest of the evening. She asked him to get food for her at the buffet and pointed to an empty spot in the corner, saying, "We can be alone over there."

Andy felt a little guilty about Lori as he brought the food back to Melissa. He supposed he should look for her and ask her to join them. Lori was a lot shyer at things like this, and she didn't know many people. Generally, Lori took things seriously, while he could usually get through anything with a joke and a smile. But he couldn't see Lori anywhere, and she probably wouldn't want to eat with them anyway.

Melissa didn't seem to notice that he turned his head to look around the room from time to time. She was talking about the play she'd been in last year. As Melissa talked, Andy remembered seeing the play. He remembered thinking that Melissa had hammed up the part. But he wondered if he'd been too critical. Anyway, that was last spring, and now it was August. The play seemed unimportant. What was important now was the way Melissa kept looking at him with those blue eyes. He felt almost hypnotized by the blue eye shadow and the dark beads of mascara at the end of her eyelashes. She looked as though she had dark rainbows around her eyes.

A five-piece orchestra was playing old-fashioned, corny music. It was the kind of music that he and Lori had always made fun of, but now it didn't seem so corny. He slipped an arm around Melissa's waist and led her to the floor. Though he had never danced before, he managed not to step on Melissa's feet too often and was pleased to hear Melissa comment that he danced very well. Perhaps he could really learn to enjoy it! He was almost sorry when the musicians took a break and he and Melissa went to the punch bowl. When Melissa excused herself for a few minutes, Andy had a chance to look around at the other guests.

There were approximately two hundred people. During the last three months, he'd heard endless conversations about the size of the wedding guest list, where to hold the reception, what to serve, and whether or not to have a band. If he'd heard his father say once, "At least I'm not paying for this," he'd heard it a hundred times.

He spotted his mother and father dancing with each other. His mother, who usually wore her long gray hair pulled back in a ponytail, had piled her hair on top of her head. Tendrils curled around her face. She looked pretty, though a bit stiff, in her high-heeled sandals and mint-green crepe dress.

His parents were laughing and talking. Andy wondered if they were having a good time. They usually wore Levi's and tee shirts when they were at home or working in their health food store. It seemed strange to see them so dressed up. Andy laughed as he remembered what his mother said when the bride's mother asked her to wear a long lace dress. His mother did have a way of expressing herself so that there could be no misunderstanding!

Melissa was gone a long time, and Andy began to get more and more uncomfortable. Here he was at his brother's wedding, dancing and flirting with a girl he'd always thought was a phony. It was exciting, and he was enjoying himself, but he was beginning to feel uneasy and a little dishonest. It was as though he was acting someone else's part in a movie.

When Melissa returned from the ladies' room, she took the cup of punch from Andy and said, "Oh, it's getting dark outside. Let's go out and look at the sunset together. Wouldn't that be wonderful?"

Andy followed Melissa out onto the balcony, and she leaned against his shoulder. "You're so tall," she said. "Tall, dark, and handsome."

Before he could respond, she went on, "Isn't it a shame we're in Cape Cod, not

California? In California they have great sunsets. All pink and gold and red—all at the same time."

Andy felt silly standing on a balcony looking at a sunset. The feeling of being an actor returned and was intensified by the setting. He just didn't feature himself in the role of romantic hero in some corny romantic movie, and yet that was obviously what Melissa expected from him. He felt as though he'd forgotten his lines.

He was glad to get back inside to the dance floor and even happier when Joe Robbins came over and asked Melissa to dance.

Melissa turned to him and asked, "Do you mind?"

"Of course not," Andy said. Again, his reaction to Melissa's words was discomfort. How many times had he, his parents, and Lori hooted in laughter at such old-fashioned dialogue? He could almost hear his mother saying, "Women are not property, so they don't have to ask a man's permission to dance with anyone else."

While Melissa danced with Joe, Andy decided to go back onto the balcony for a minute. The room was stuffy with cigarette smoke, and he wanted some fresh air. He leaned against the railing, looking at the tail end of the sunset. He was surprised when, all of a sudden, he heard Lori's voice calling from the dark shadows.

Lori said in a high, squeaky voice, "Oh, Andy, California sunsets are just too thrilling!"

Andy turned and grabbed Lori's arm. "Where have you been all afternoon? I looked everywhere for you."

"No you didn't," Lori said. "I've been watching you. You spent all your time with Melissa." She shoved Andy away from her and stepped out of the darkness into the light shining through the ballroom window.

"Why didn't you come rescue me? Melissa has been leading me around all day as though she owned me," he complained.

Lori laughed. It was a deep, round, full laugh. Andy realized that, of all the things he liked about his friend, her laugh was the best.

"Why should I rescue you? You know you loved it. You've been having a wonderful time," she teased.

Andy pinned Lori's arms up against

the wall and shook his head in mock anger as he asked, "What's a friend for?"

Lori laughed again and leaned her head back, looking up at the sky as she imitated Melissa's voice again. "Oh, Andy, the sunset is soooo thrilling!"

Andy leaned forward, and he suddenly felt a sharp, unfamiliar excitement. Suddenly he wanted to kiss her just below the chin where the dark shadows lay. The hollow of her neck seemed irresistible. He took a deep breath, and let Lori go. "What's the matter?" she asked.

"I don't know," Andy said. How could he ever explain to Lori what he was feeling? He didn't understand it himself. All he knew was that for one terrible minute, he had wanted more than anything in the world to hold Lori in his arms and kiss her. He said, "Maybe I ate too much cake. Maybe I should go home."

"And leave Melissa all alone?" Lori teased.

"It's not funny," Andy answered sharply.

Lori's face straightened immediately, and she said, "I'll drive you."

"No." Andy shook his head. "I can drive myself."

"But you came with your folks," Lori pointed out in a practical manner. "If I borrow their car and drive you home, I can bring the car back to the party."

Andy stepped back and looked at Lori quizzically. What had actually happened? He'd felt a desire to kiss her—so what? It wasn't the end of the world. Anyone could have feelings like that. The important thing was not to panic and say something dumb. Lori would be horrified if he told her how he was really feeling.

"I'm fine now," he said. "I guess I overdosed on sugar."

Lori laughed. "You can't spend all your life on carob cookies and mint tea and then not have a reaction to this gooey stuff. Anyway"—her voice changed—"here comes your girlfriend, but remember, if you want a ride, I'm your woman."

"She's not my girlfriend," Andy said quickly. Why had he snapped at Lori? It wasn't her fault he'd wanted to kiss her. He was already over his temporary insanity. Now he would go back to the party and flirt like crazy with Melissa.

3

The next morning Melissa called to see if Andy would go with her to a beach party that night. "I wanted to call you earlier, but I wasn't sure my folks would let me out. They're angry with me about some old thing or other all the time these days," she explained, her voice soft and breathless.

"I know what you mean," Andy said. "Mom got mad at me last week because I didn't fold the paper bags right. It cost me two days' work around the house. When she gets angry, it's an automatic sentence to hard labor." He was flattered that Melissa had called. What would she be like if he got to know her? Really know her, the way he knew Lori?

Finally, he admitted, "The truth is, I told Lori I'd go fishing with her." As he told Melissa this, he was seeing Lori in his mind as she'd appeared at the reception. She was wearing that yellow dress, and her soft brown hair curled around her face. She'd been the same old Lori and yet different. Maybe he didn't really know Lori any better than he did Melissa. The thought was disquieting.

"If you have a date with someone else . . ."

"It's not a date," Andy answered quickly. "I hang out with Lori all the time. You know that."

"Yes, I do," Melissa answered. "I just didn't know it was so serious."

"It's not serious," Andy protested, annoyed. "It's just that I promised Lori I'd go with her. We always go fishing on Saturday night. It's the best time."

"Bring Lori along," Melissa suggested. "We're all going to Pilgrim Lake Beach. If you think she'll get bored, she can even bring her fishing pole with her."

Andy sighed and answered, "Well, I'll ask her, but I don't think that Lori wants to go to Pilgrim Lake."

"The least you can do is ask her," Melissa insisted. "I'll call you back in about an hour to hear what she has to say."

Not understanding how he'd gotten himself into this predicament, Andy heard himself agreeing before he dropped the receiver onto the hook. He dialed Lori's number. Soon he heard her cheerful voice saying, "Valentino here."

"Hi Lori," Andy said. "You still want to go fishing tonight?"

"Sure," Lori answered. "We always go fishing on Saturday night."

"Well, I thought maybe you'd like to do something different," Andy said quickly. "Maybe you'd like to go to a beach party at Pilgrim Lake with Melissa Gaylord and a lot of kids."

He was surprised at how anxious he felt as he waited for Lori's answer.

"You go to the party, Andy. I'm going to stay home and watch television."

"Watch television?" Andy asked. "You hate TV. Come on, you'll have a good time." He hated the insistence in his voice. In the first place, he wasn't sure he really wanted Lori, and in the second place, he wasn't sure he really wanted to go. Fishing would probably be more fun.

"I don't want to go to a sappy old beach party with you and Melissa," Lori said. "You go. You'll have a good time."

"I don't want to go without you."

"Sure you do," Lori said. "You're dying to go without me. That's all right, Andy. We can go fishing next week if you don't have a date with Melissa."

"Oh come on, Lori. Don't be like that," Andy said. But Lori had already hung up. Andy stood for a moment listening to the dial tone buzz in his ear.

Usually, on Saturdays Andy worked for his folks, but today they were doing the budget, so he wasn't wanted. When his mother and father did the financial planning for the store, they negotiated every decision. There had been much less money since they had given up their regular jobs, but they were both happier.

His mother and father were still working on the books when he came into the shop. They sat at one of the small metal tables near the produce bins. Each of them had a cup of herbal tea in big mugs. When Andy entered, they looked up and, seeing it wasn't a customer, went on with their conversation.

"Hi, what's for supper?" Andy asked. He was already munching on some roasted cashews from the bin in front of him.

"There's vegetable soup in the pot," his mother said. "And some guacamole for salad."

"You still fighting over money?" Andy teased.

"Your father and I are not fighting over money," his mother answered. "We are discussing plans for the future."

His father smiled. "Go ahead and eat, son. Doing books with your mother makes me long for the good old days when a man was boss."

"Humph," Andy's mother said. Then she went back to the business at hand. "I think it's silly to stock so many vitamins when we're getting requests for cookbooks."

"But the vitamin business is repeat business," his father answered.

Andy could tell that this was a continuation of an old conversation and that they would be happier if he stayed out of it. The store was a family business, but he was a very junior partner in the corporation. For him, it was a way to earn spending money, but for his folks, it was their life work. He went over to the counter and lifted the soup pot lid.

After he finished the soup and some rye crackers, he ate some yogurt and a banana with two handfuls of trail mix. That would hold him for a while, at least until the beach party. There would be potato chips, hot dogs, and other junk food that his folks thought was a fate worse than death. But Andy had long ago learned that the best policy was to eat the way his folks did at home and eat whatever he wanted when he was with his friends. Tim wouldn't do that, so he and his mother carried on a constant argument about diet and nutrition. Ruth was sure Tim was going to live a short and unhealthy life because he liked to eat at McDonald's. Tim called his folks' food ideas "fads."

Andy had an easier attitude toward food. He liked the supper that he'd just finished and didn't mind eating the food that the store sold. At the same time, he liked the way his friends ate and figured it wouldn't hurt him to eat the way they did at least some of the time. He wished his mother and Tim could learn to relax a little bit about diet and lots of other things. I'm more like Dad, Andy thought, and the idea surprised him. Was Tim like his mother? Their differences were so strong, but maybe they were a lot alike. Both of them were outspoken and opinionated. That was for sure.

After he finished eating, he took his dishes over to the sink to wash them. He said, "I'm going to the beach party with Melissa Gaylord." He tried to keep his voice even and not attach too much importance to his statement.

"That the blonde with the blue eyes?" his father asked.

"The blue eye shadow," his mother said. "I think her eyes are green, really."

"Sounds as though you're the one with green eyes," his father said.

His mother flushed and said, "You think I'd be jealous of a sixteen-year-old?"

Andy was surprised by the sharpness of his mother's tone. "Hey, Ma, you don't have to be jealous of anyone— ever," he said.

His mother laughed. "And I thought I had liberated you two men! Thanks for the vote of confidence, anyway. And have a good time."

Andy knew he was early when he drove up to the Gaylords' door, but he couldn't think of any place to go. He thought it would look funny to sit outside, so he knocked on the door and said, "Hi, Mrs. Gaylord, I guess I'm early."

"Yes, you are," Mrs. Gaylord answered cheerfully. "And Melissa is usually late. Maybe you ought to come and chat with her father and me."

Andy groaned inwardly as he realized what he'd let himself in for. Now he'd have to spend fifteen minutes talking with Mr. and Mrs. Gaylord about the wedding. Andy followed Mrs. Gaylord into the living room where Mr. Gaylord was reading the paper. Sure enough, they wanted to talk about how pretty his brother's wedding had been. Andy was relieved to find that Melissa's mother talked as much as she did. He spent the next twenty-five minutes saying, "Yes, it seems that way," or "No, I don't think so." Mrs. Gaylord did the rest.

When Melissa came into the living room, it was twenty minutes after they'd agreed he would pick her up. She said, "Why Andy, imagine seeing you here!"

Andy didn't know what to say to that, and so he said nothing at all, but Melissa didn't seem to expect much conversation from him. She kept up a running patter as she loaded Andy down with a basket of food, sweaters, and a blanket. As they walked to the car, she was talking about buying a swimsuit on sale. Then she switched to what classes she hoped to get into next semester.

Andy relaxed and concentrated on his driving, since Melissa was carrying the burden of the conversation. He drove the car through the old town of Orleans onto Monument Road, which stretched and curved past the wonderful old Cape Cod houses. He took Herring Brook Road to the delightful little cove where the party would be. Parking in the public lot, Andy and Melissa carried their food past the picnic tables to the fine sandy beach where the other kids waited. It was a beautiful night, and the full moon made the water look like a jewel shimmering under the dark blue sky.

Melissa waved to everyone, and then showed Andy where to spread their blanket. Most of the kids at the party were friends of Melissa's, not Andy's. He recognized several of the guys. Melissa and Andy sat down on the blanket, and Melissa started telling some of the others about her day. Andy sat quietly, listening to her and the others laugh and joke. He had noticed that other guys had looked at him with respect when he'd walked up with her. He could see their faces in the moonlight, and their expressions were a mixture of deference and envy. Andy decided it was fun to date such a popular girl.

Most of the kids were drinking beer, and Andy was glad that Melissa didn't drink. It made it easier for him, and no one asked him why he was drinking soft drinks. In fact, no one seemed to notice or care.

After about an hour, Melissa and a couple of the other girls walked up the street to call one of the girls' mothers.

The minute they were out of hearing

distance, Joe asked Andy, "How come you didn't bring Lori tonight?"

"She didn't want to come," Andy said.

"Too bad."

Andy realized that he missed Lori. If Lori had been there, the whole party would have been different. It was a little like having his shadow missing. He hadn't thought about Lori until Joe mentioned her, but now he wished very much that she were here.

When Melissa and the other two girls came back, Andy tried to get her to dig for clams, but she said she didn't want to. Some of the boys joined him, but the girls all chose to stay by the fire and try to boil some water in case they found enough clams to cook.

They found no clams. The evening had grown chilly, and Andy was glad he'd worn his heavy sweater. But when he got back to the fire, he had to take his sweater off and give it to Melissa, who was shivering and complaining but wouldn't put on the jeans she'd brought, saying she wanted to enjoy the beach. Andy wondered if she were wearing her swimsuit because she looked so good in it.

She stood hugging herself by the fire and said through chattering teeth, "Andy Johnson, you haven't paid any attention to me at all tonight. Now come over here by the fire and talk to me."

He wanted to tell Melissa that she hadn't given him a chance to say anything to her. But instead, he smiled and picked up a sandwich from the picnic supper. Biting into the tuna salad, he said, "This is good."

"Eat some of each kind and tell me which ones you like best," Melissa said.

"Tell you what, I'll eat them all if you'll put on your jeans. Okay?"

Melissa looked as if she wanted to argue, but then she nodded and said, "If you insist. But I'm not cold." But she scrambled into the Levi's and came back to sit beside him on the blanket.

It was growing dark. A full moon hung low in a star-studded sky. The wind had died down, and Andy could hear the gentle slapping of the water against the shore above the soft whispers of the other couples. He slipped his arm around Melissa's shoulder and drew her closer. She leaned against him and lifted her face for his kiss.

Sometime later Andy surreptitiously looked at his watch. Eleven-thirty! He had promised his parents to be home by midnight. Now he would be late. The time had passed all too quickly. He had to admit that he had found kissing Melissa more interesting than listening to her talk. She might be pretty and popular, but he found her boring. They'd been together for four hours, and she hadn't talked about anything that interested him. He suspected that Melissa always talked about what interested Melissa. He made up his mind that he wouldn't ask her out again. At least, not soon. He decided it might be a good idea to start dating more, though.

Andy drove to Melissa's house and parked in her driveway. Then he said, "Thanks, Melissa. I had a good time."

Melissa smiled up at him, then leaned forward and kissed him. "I had a nice time too, Andy. Will you call me tomorrow?"

Andy gulped and searched for the right words. How could he explain that he didn't want to take her out again without hurting her feelings? He couldn't. A thousand words raced through his head, but when he opened his mouth, only one word croaked out. "Yes."

"What time?" Melissa asked. "I want to be sure and be home."

Andy felt his heart sink. Now he'd done it. Now he was committed to calling Melissa again. How had he been so dumb? "About two o'clock."

"That's wonderful," Melissa said. "I was going over to Suzanne's at four, but I would have waited for your call. You know, Andy, I've wanted to go out with you for a long time. You're so handsome and . . . I just thought you would be as nice as you are. Good night." She kissed him again quickly and opened the car door.

With a sinking feeling, he watched her enter her house.

4

When Andy awoke in the morning, his first thought was of Melissa and the promise he'd made to her to call her. He groaned and rolled over and pulled the pillow over his head. How had he managed to get himself into such a predicament? He didn't want Melissa for a girlfriend.

He tried very hard to go back to sleep during the next thirty minutes, but all he succeeded in doing was spending thirty minutes worrying about what he was going to say to her. He had just about given up on the idea of going back to sleep when his mother called him and said that Lori was on the phone.

At the thought of Lori, his stomach took another one of those surprising flip-flops, and he jumped out of bed to race to the telephone. Maybe Lori could help him. Maybe there was something that Lori could do to get Melissa off his back. But Lori wanted him to go for a bike ride with her and Mary Lynne.

Mary Lynne was the little girl Lori volunteered to spend time with as a part of the Little Sister program. When Lori decided to volunteer to be a "big sister," Andy had been a little surprised. He'd never thought of Lori as being the type who was particularly good with kids. But Lori took her responsibility very seriously and spent at least six hours a week with Mary Lynne. Sometimes, Lori invited him to go along, but usually she thought it was better to give Mary Lynne her undivided attention.

"I'd like to go," Andy said. "How's Mary Lynne doing?"

"She's still not talking much. I mean, she talks a little bit about what we're doing, but she doesn't talk at all about her family or how she's feeling."

"Didn't they tell you not to expect too much?"

"Yes. But I don't think it's expecting too much to want a seven-year-old to tell me a little bit about what she's thinking. How am I going to help her if I don't know what's going on with her?"

"You're helping her just by spending time with her. I thought that was the point."

"Maybe." Lori sounded doubtful about it. Then, obviously trying to look on the bright side of things, she said, "Anyway, she seems to be getting over some of her fear of men. At least, she likes you. Mary Lynne was the one who wanted to invite you."

Andy discovered that he was feeling just a little disappointed that the invitation had been Mary Lynne's idea, not Lori's.

By the time Andy had finished breakfast, Lori and Mary Lynne were at the door. Lori was wearing some old white painter Levi's that were covered with purple and blue spots of ink, remnants from last year's work on the props for the senior play. She wore a bright yellow sweatshirt with the words I'M DE-SIRABLE written across the front.

Andy looked up from his bowl of cereal and asked, "Why don't you get rid of that sweatshirt? It's corny."

Lori laughed. She reached out and

pulled a lock of his straight brown hair. "I like this sweatshirt. It's got personality."

"It's corny," Andy said. He reached over to pull Mary Lynne's pigtails. "How's tricks, ML?" he asked.

Mary Lynne looked up at him and grinned. The space where her two front teeth belonged was still open, but Andy saw that new teeth were beginning to come through. He asked, "You ready to go a long way today, kiddo?"

Mary Lynne nodded her head enthusiastically. Lori frowned. "I thought we'd just go down to the Nauset Beach and back. Don't want to tire her out."

"You act like an old lady, Lori. Mary Lynne can take it. Let's go over to Money Head. We can look for Captain Kidd's gold, the way we did when we were ML's age."

"I'm not going to wear the kid out, Andy. We'll go to Nauset Beach. That's far enough."

Andy didn't argue. After all, Lori was the one who'd taken on Mary Lynne as a project. It was none of his business.

Lori led the bicycle caravan down Andy's street and onto Route 28. As soon as she could, she got them off the busy highway and onto one of the winding side streets that circled around the lovely gray-shingled houses with their beautifully landscaped yards. Though it was too late for roses, many of the yards still sported geraniums and impatiens. Some people had already put in their chrysanthemums, and everywhere the hydrangea bushes were blooming. The road wound around, dipping and turning to give tantalizing views of the ocean. Andy loved bicycling in Orleans. He couldn't imagine ever moving away.

They rode for about an hour. When they got to Nauset Beach, Lori pulled up to the bicycle stand and parked her bike. Turning to Andy, she said, "We could get something to eat here. Maybe take it down to the beach."

Andy reached his hand into his pocket, pulling out five dollars. He said, "Here, I've got some cash left."

Lori grinned. "You mean you didn't spend it all on that blonde last night?"

Andy ignored the crack and walked toward the take-out restaurant at the bottom of the landing. Lori and Mary Lynne followed him. When Lori chipped in the two dollars and change that she had in her Levi's pockets, there was enough money for cheeseburgers and French fries for all three of them. They carried the food down to the water's edge and sat on the sand munching.

Mary Lynne finished first and walked down to the public water fountain for a drink. Then she sat down in the sand and began to scoop up handfuls of wet sand. She picked up an old cup and filled it with sand, turning the cup upside down for sand cupcakes.

Lori asked Andy, "You have a good time last night?"

"It would've been better with you there," Andy answered.

Lori didn't say anything to that, only turned her body slightly so that she could watch Mary Lynne playing on the water's edge.

Andy said, "Melissa's nice."

Lori nodded. "I figured you thought so."

Andy tried again. "She talks a lot."

"She sure does."

"But sometimes that's okay," Andy said. "It makes it easier somehow."

"Easier?" Lori asked.

"Well, you know. Easier to make conversation."

Lori laughed again, and Andy was delighted once again by the wonderful sound. "Don't you mean it's easier *not* to make conversation?"

Andy leaned over and picked up a handful of the warm sand, which he let dribble through his fingers as he said slowly, "She asked me to call her today. I said I would."

Lori nodded her head quickly as though that was perfectly natural and not very interesting. Then she called out to Mary Lynne, "Come on, ML. It's time to get going." Then Lori jumped up and brushed the sand off the back of her painter's Levi's.

Andy stood up as well and asked, "You don't care, do you?"

Lori turned toward him as she asked, "Care? Why should I care?"

He shrugged and said, "Well, I don't know. I just thought, her being a girl, and your being a girl and all . . ."

His voice trailed off, and Lori looked at him in superior amusement as she said, "I don't care who you date. You're a free agent."

"Yeah, I guess I am," Andy said to the wind as he watched Lori turn and walk back toward the edge of the beach where their bicycles were parked. Andy began to run across the sand to catch up with Lori and Mary Lynne. He ran over, grabbed Mary Lynne around the waist, lifted her high in the air, and swung her around, holding on tight to her waist as he shouted, "You're a bird, you're a plane, you're a super-brain. Whee-e-e! Mary Lynne. Fly through the air."

"Put her down!" Lori said sharply, but Andy kept swinging. He was still swinging when Lori came over and grabbed his arm, throwing him slightly off balance so that he almost dropped Mary Lynne. As he staggered, Lori grabbed Mary Lynne around the waist and pulled her tightly to her; looking over Mary Lynne's head, she said to Andy in a fierce voice, "You know that scares her, Andy. Why do you do it?"

"It doesn't scare her," Andy protested. "She likes it, don't you, Mary Lynne?" Mary Lynne clutched Lori's waist.

Andy bent over and said, "Hey, honey, I didn't mean to hurt you. I wouldn't hurt you, you know that, don't you?"

Lori's eyes were blazing as she held Mary Lynne close to her. She said to Andy fiercely, "I've asked you not to scare her! If you're going to come with us on these bike rides, you're going to have to do what I say."

Lori's words made Andy so angry that he had to bite his lip to keep from saying something he would be sorry about. He didn't want to quarrel with Lori in front of Mary Lynne. He searched his mind for the words to defend himself without alarming Mary Lynne.

Finally he said, "There's no sense trying to talk to you when you get like this, Lori. I don't know what's happening to you. You used to be a really easygoing person, but lately it seems that all you ever do is snap, crackle, and pop."

Lori didn't laugh. Her dark brown eyebrows were knitted close in a frown, and her blue eyes seemed to be sending sparks. "And you think you can turn everything away with a joke, Andy. I'm sick of your jokes, and I'm sick of your scaring Mary Lynne."

"Maybe you'd like to be alone?" Andy said.

"Maybe I would," Lori snapped back.

They stood and looked at each other; neither of them seemed to be able to find the words to bridge the gap that was widening between them.

Mary Lynne was still clinging to Lori's waist, but she reached one hand out to Andy and said in small voice, "I wasn't scared, Andy. Honest, I wasn't." Andy felt more guilty than ever.

He patted her arm, saying, "I was just trying to have some fun, ML. I won't do it anymore."

"Just don't forget again, Andy. This isn't the first time," Lori said fiercely.

Somehow the fact that Lori wasn't ready to let bygones be bygones made Andy angry all over again. He had to clench his fists to keep from reaching out and socking her one. Instead, he said coldly, "We'd better get back now. I have to call Melissa at two."

On Andy's second date with Melissa, they went to a movie and then over to Joe Robbins's house, where they watched television until midnight. Joe and a girl named Ann were watching an old movie as they ate pizza and talked about school. Andy yawned a few times, but he managed to stay awake.

That night, when Melissa asked if he would call her tomorrow, Andy said, "I'll be busy tomorrow."

"Okay," Melissa said. "I'll call you on Monday." Then she kissed him lightly and opened the door of the car to go into the house.

Melissa called him on Monday, and he told his father to say he was busy and would call her back. She called again on Tuesday. That time, he made his mother say he'd gone out. She didn't call on Wednesday, and Andy breathed a sigh of relief. Maybe she'd gotten the message and wouldn't call anymore. But on Thursday, she called him at the health food store, and his mother motioned him to come to the telephone. Andy shook his head and said, "Tell her I'm not here."

"No."

"Tell her I'll call her later."

His mother nodded, but when she put the receiver down, she said, "This is it! That's the last time I'll lie for you to that poor girl."

"She's the one who keeps calling," Andy pointed out. "So why is she a poor girl? Besides, you don't like her."

"Call her," his father said from across the store where he was putting nuts into bins.

Andy went to the telephone and dialed Melissa's number, but when he asked for her, her mother said she was out for the afternoon.

"Talk to her tomorrow," his father ordered. "It's not fair to your mother to keep this game up."

"What do I say?"

"Tell her the truth," his mother suggested.

Andy laughed. "Sure, I can hear it now—'Melissa, I don't answer your calls because you're boring.'"

"Find the words," his father said. "Tell her you're dating Lori."

"I'm not!"

"Maybe you should be," his father said. "At least I never heard you call her boring."

* * *

"Tim's coming over for supper," Andy's mother said. She made a wry face and added, "I offered to cook meat loaf, but they said eggplant Parmesan would be fine."

Andy laughed. "Maybe Tim's tired of Patricia's cooking."

His mother shook her head. "I can hear them now—they're coming over because it's time. They'll always do the proper thing, and it's proper to have dinner with one's parents. I think we can expect them once a month—exactly."

Andy wished there were something he could do to help his mother understand that Tim had a right to choose his life, just as she had chosen her own. But his mother would never understand her oldest son's choices. As far as she was concerned, Tim didn't make choices, he just stood still.

At supper that night, Andy thought Tim looked happy. He had put on a little weight and seemed more easygoing. Andy decided he liked Patricia, even though she had asked him several times about his relationship with Melissa. He was not ready to talk about that yet, and certainly couldn't tell her that he found her cousin boring and wanted to drop her.

After dinner Tim suggested a walk to Andy.

"Do that, boys," Mrs. Johnson said. "It will give me a good chance to visit with Pat."

"Mom's planning a consciousness-raising session," Tim said. "I'm sure she'll tell Pat to insist on my doing my full share of the housework!" He picked up his jacket and followed Andy to the street.

"Mom said I should talk to you," Tim said. "Trouble?"

"Girls," Andy said. "Melissa keeps calling me on the phone, and I don't know how to get rid of her."

"And Mom wants me to tell Patricia to tell her?" Tim's voice sounded incredulous.

"No. She just thought you might have some good advice. She said you had girls after you all the time in high school."

Tim laughed. "Some. Usually, I just was polite and stalled until they lost interest."

"I'm not sure that will work," Andy said.

"She seemed okay," Tim said. "You're not interested?"

"I could never be serious about her."

"Do you have to be?" Tim asked. "You're not supposed to be serious at sixteen. You're supposed to play the field. What does Lori think?"

"We're not talking. We had a fight."

"About Melissa?"

"No," Andy answered. "We're just fighting. Seems like everything I do is wrong. You'd think that I could do something to please her once in a while, but I don't know; things just aren't the same between Lori and me."

"You're upset about Lori, huh kid?"

"Yeah. I don't have any other really close friends, you know. I mean, I've got a lot of the guys at school, and they're okay to hang around with and everything, but Lori and me . . . Well . . . Yeah . . . I miss her."

"Maybe you should call her up and apologize," Tim suggested.

"Apologize!" Andy shouted into the cold summer wind. I'm not going to apologize when I'm not wrong. I haven't done anything to Lori."

"Then why is she so mad?" Tim asked.

"I don't know! It just seems as if every little thing makes her mad lately. She's just not the same." Suddenly, Lori's face floated across his mind. He could see her as clearly as if she were standing right there, walking down the dark street with him. He said, "Maybe it isn't just Lori that's changing. Maybe I'm changing, too."

"Did it ever occur to you to date Lori?" Tim asked.

Andy stopped and stared at his brother. He flushed and said, "Lori's not the same kind of girl as Melissa. She's not interested in dating and boys."

"Are you sure?"

"Sure, I'm sure. She never goes out on dates."

"Maybe the right guy hasn't asked her," Tim suggested. When Andy didn't respond, Tim asked, "You don't think friends should date each other? Is that it?"

"I certainly can't date Lori!" Andy protested.

"Why not?"

"How could I date Lori? We're on the same baseball team!"

"Lori's a girl, isn't she?"

"Yes."

"And you like her a lot?"

"That doesn't prove anything!"

"Maybe not," Tim said, "but it seems to me Lori's perfect for you."

"No," Andy said. "It wouldn't work." He was sorry that the conversation had taken this turn. Tim's idea that he should date Lori was silly. Andy wished that he had never brought up the subject of girls with Tim. The two brothers walked back to the house in silence.

Andy woke with a start. He turned on the light and stared out the window at the oak tree outside. He had been dreaming about Lori. In his dream he was leaning forward to kiss her when he suddenly realized who she was. He had awakened before he had had a chance to carry out his plan. But the feeling persisted. He still wanted to kiss Lori! That was the problem! No wonder he didn't want to date Melissa! His brother had been right after all.

He looked around his room, at the bright yellow walls, at the picture of the fourth-grade Little League team on his bureau. From a distance he could just make out Lori. She was smiling, her arms raised to signal their victory. He was beside her waving his baseball cap in celebration.

It was as plain as the nose on his face. He was in love with Lori. And there was nothing he could do about it except hope that he would get over it quickly. Telling her was out of the question. She would just laugh. She would think him a fool. He might lose her as a friend. He would forever feel uncomfortable with her.

With a sigh, he turned off the light and snuggled down under his covers. There was no point thinking about it. Soon he fell into a deep, dreamless sleep.

5

Lori called Andy at six-thirty the next morning. Her voice sounded so distant and far away that Andy's first question to her was, "Where are you?"

"Under the covers," Lori answered. "Mom always says it's too early to call people before nine, but I knew you'd be up."

"That's right," Andy said. He tried to keep his voice light and casual. "What's up?"

"I thought you might like to go for a bike ride today. Just the two of us," Lori said. "We haven't done anything alone for a long time."

"You're right," Andy said. There was a long silence as he waited to see what she would say next.

"Anyway, I thought we might ride

our bikes together—just the two of us, like the old days," she added.

"Great," Andy replied. But he knew that the trip wouldn't be exactly like the old days. He wished with all his heart that he could turn time backward and that he and Lori could be friends and nothing more, the way they used to be. But time didn't roll backward just because you wanted it to, and he was going to have to work on getting his emotions under control. Maybe this bike ride would help. "I'll be over in half an hour," Andy said and hung up the telephone.

After a fast breakfast, Andy pedaled to Lori's house and stopped his bicycle just outside her window. Bending over to pick up some small pebbles, he tossed them lightly against her window as a signal that he was here. Lori's mother like to sleep late when she wasn't working, and he didn't want to wake her. Sometimes, Mrs. Valentino got cranky and decided that Lori had to stay in the house and work. It was easier just to bypass the doorbell.

Lori was downstairs in a second, and Andy asked, "Want to go all the way to P.T.?"

"To Provincetown?" Lori asked. "It's an all-day trip."

"Fun though," Andy answered, and Lori grinned at him in agreement.

She unlocked her bicycle from the chain around the radiator in the back hallway of the apartment building, and they were on the road.

As they pedaled down the highway toward Provincetown, Andy enjoyed looking at the small shops that lined the highway. All of the restaurants seemed to advertise the same menus of lobster and crab, and it seemed to Andy that every little shop was either selling shells or pillows of satin with the words CAPE COD embroidered on them.

He followed Lori, watching the way her body seemed to bend with the wind as though she were a part of the natural landscape. She was wearing the yellow sweatshirt again—the one that said, I'M DESIRABLE. The words seemed like a bitter joke to Andy. Watching her weave and dart through the traffic, he thought that she was as beautiful as anyone he had ever seen. Her long slim legs seemed to fit onto the bicycle as though they were a natural part of the mechanism. Lori was a born athlete, and he hoped that someday she would get a chance at a professional ball team. She didn't seem to care much, saying she'd be happy to end up a phys ed teacher. There was a time when they'd dreamed they'd both be playing for the Dodgers, but those were childish dreams. Andy knew he'd never make pro ball. But Lori had a chance at a women's team if she wanted it badly enough.

Andy slipped into a daydream in which he was watching Lori hit her first home run of the season. He was watching her round the bases and come in to home plate. Then she ran over and threw her arms around him. He pedaled furiously to clear his mind of such nonsense.

Overtaking her, he called out, "Come on, lazy bones," as he passed her. For the next hour he set the pace, making them move faster than usual; but it felt good to urge his body against the wind and stretch his endurance close to his limit. He didn't look around to see if Lori was behind him because he knew she could keep up. Finally he heard her calling out to him, "Hey, let's rest."

Andy smiled. He'd been able to out-pedal Lori. He slowed down as they entered the town of Provincetown and let Lori take the lead again. She turned off Route 6A, and they pedaled onto the narrow, one-laned Commercial Street that was the heart and center of Provincetown.

They went past the Provincetown theater, and the small Church of St. Mary with its beautiful front courtyard. Though Andy had been here many times, he always enjoyed seeing the brightly painted shops with their quaint architecture.

But it wasn't only the shops with their brightly painted signs that clamored for attention. Artists and tourists seemed to be in a contest with each other for the most colorful costumes. Andy saw one man who must have been in his seventies, wearing a bright red shirt with brighter purple pants. He had a chartreuse sweater slung across his shoulders and was carrying a gold-headed cane, which he swung forward as an aid for his brisk sneakered stride.

Andy and Lori rode past McMillan Wharf, where tourists began their deep-sea fishing and harbor tours. Then they circled back to Commercial Street and over to Cottage Street and the crest of

Chip Hill. They stopped for a few minutes to look at the place where workmen found the old stones that were supposed to be part of a wall built by Norsemen over a thousand years ago.

"Let's go get something to eat," Lori said.

Andy agreed quickly, and they bought sandwiches to take out to the Province Lands where they would picnic. As they waited for their sandwiches, Andy shivered and said, "Maybe we should eat inside. It's getting cold."

"It's still September," Lori said.

Andy laughed. "September—July—so what? I'll bet it's down to forty degrees."

"I like to eat on the dunes," Lori answered. "It is so beautiful there."

Andy ordered a cup of coffee to drink while they waited for the sandwiches. That would warm him up. Lori said she wasn't cold and had a Coke.

They pedaled out to Province Lands very quickly. Once there, they found a bicycle trail that took them over the starkly beautiful stretches of sand dunes and beaches. It was a cold day, and they didn't see many people on bicycles. They soon were far enough away from the Visitors' Center to feel as though they were totally alone.

Andy enjoyed the lonely stretches of dunes and watching the bright blue sea, but he was hungry, cold, and getting tired. Sometimes Lori got carried away when she got started on a ride like this. When the sun went under the clouds and the wind from the beach turned even cooler, Andy called out, "Hey, let's turn around."

But Lori was getting off her bike now and calling out to him, "I want to see that old lighthouse over there."

Andy looked at the remaining ruins of the old stone lighthouse about a mile down on the beach. He protested, "You've seen it before. Nothing there. Just some old boards and stones. And trash. Remember?"

"I promised Mary Lynne I'd bring her a shell," Lori said and took off her shoes. She put her shoes beside her bicycle and started out over the soft, white sand. Andy followed.

The wind was really blowing now, and there were whitecaps flashing across the dark blue water. Andy wished that he'd worn a stocking cap and sweater instead of this lightweight windbreaker. And Lori looked frozen in her yellow sweatshirt.

They walked toward the water's edge. Andy had his arms crossed in front of him; he wanted to complain about the cold, but he hated to do anything to make trouble between them. In the old days, Andy thought bitterly, I would have said whatever came to my mind. Now I'm scared of saying the wrong thing all the time.

As though she had read his thought, Lori said, "You're sure quiet today. What's the matter?"

"Nothing," Andy answered.

"Look at those waves!" Lori said, pointing to the rough whitecaps on the ocean's surface.

"Going to storm," Andy replied. His words were immediately reinforced by a loud crack of thunder and a far-off flash of lightning.

Lori bent down, scooped up a common clam shell, and put it in her Levi's pocket, saying, "That'll have to do. We can go now if you want."

Andy grabbed Lori's hand and said, "It doesn't matter. We're going to get wet anyway. Let's find the kid something better than that." He held her hand, and they walked down to the edge of the water. Andy bent over to pick up a small brown-and-white speckled shell. He placed it in Lori's hand. He ignored the second rumble of thunder and pointed to a white object farther down the beach.

"We'd better go back. It's going to rain," Lori said.

But Andy began to run forward, dragging Lori by the hand. When they picked up the next shell, he saw one even farther down the beach. "This is crazy, Andy," Lori protested.

The rain started. At first it was a small, soft patter of cold rain. It flowed down from the sky, hit their heads, and ran in small rivers down their heads and necks, making a soft, wet sponge of their jacket collars.

"This is awful! We'd better go," Lori said.

Andy nodded and turned to point toward the lighthouse ruins. They started running.

By now the wind was whipping up the waves, and the sky was almost black except for the flashes of lightning. Andy followed Lori across the wet sand to the broken down old lighthouse. It was really no more than a heap of rocks and a rusty iron door. Lori pulled the door open, saying, "It can't be any worse inside."

"It won't be any better," Andy shouted over the storm's noise. Nevertheless, he helped her yank on the door until they managed to pull it ajar.

Lori ducked inside, and he followed. It was surprisingly dry. Lori pointed up to the beams about twelve feet over their heads. She said, "They're as good as a roof."

"If they don't fall on us," Andy said. By standing against the structure's dry wall and under the rickety old beam, they could avoid the worst part of the storm.

Lori shivered. "Maybe we could start a fire," she suggested.

Andy looked around inside the abandoned lighthouse. There were plenty of small pieces of old wood, and there was even a pile of trash over in the driest corner. Beside it there was a heap of ashes surrounded by a circle of stones. Clearly, this was not the first time that the lighthouse had been used to shelter people. He picked up a couple of dry comic books from the trash and said, "We could use these to start the fire."

Lori picked up some pieces of wood from the broken staircase. She said, "I hope no one gets us for trespassing."

"Me, too." Andy took the wood from her. He laid the kindling carefully over the crumpled comic books within the ring of stones.

Lori reached into her Levi's pocket and brought out a package of matches.

Andy said, "I've got a knife if we need it."

They used three matches before the comic books caught. Then the fire flared and blazed. Lori bent down to get as close to the small fire as she could. She held her hands over it, saying, "That's better. It's kind of cozy in here."

Andy laughed and looked around. It was circular, with a circular wooden staircase going up to the second floor. But the staircase had fallen away, and there wasn't really any second floor— just the beams and a small portion of the floor that served as their protection. He held his hands out over the fire and said, "Not exactly cozy, but better than the storm."

Water poured in on the other side of the lighthouse where there was no roof. It ran down the rocky floor toward them. Andy said to Lori, "We may have to move our fire higher—over there on the ledge—if we don't want to get wetter."

Lori looked up and saw the water was running down the sides of the rocks and across the floor of the lighthouse. "Do we have any more paper?" she asked.

"Some brown paper bags over in the corner that look dry enough," Andy said.

"We'd better get those over here right now so that they can dry out," Lori suggested.

Because they were old campers, neither Lori nor Andy had any trouble finding dry things that would burn. They laid a supply of kindling on a rocky ledge in the driest part of the lighthouse. Then they returned to the small fire, which burned merrily inside the stone circle. Andy threw down a large two-by-four board and said, "We can sit here."

Lori sat down beside him. They watched the fire dance in front of them for a few minutes.

Andy asked, "Remember the time your mom took us camping?"

Lori laughed and said, "She sure was scared, wasn't she?"

"It was nice of her, though," Andy replied. "She'd never done anything like that, and she was all alone. Your mom's a nice woman."

"So's your mom," Lori offered.

"She's having a hard time right now," Andy said.

"You mean Tim's wedding?"

"Just accepting Tim."

Lori nodded comfortably and said, "She'll work it out. I like Tim."

"Everyone likes Tim," Andy agreed.

"He and your mother are a lot alike."

Andy turned to look at Lori with interest. "Do you think that's what makes them so angry with each other?"

Lori nodded slowly and said, "Sometimes people get angry with people they're close to."

They sat silently for a while longer, and then Andy turned toward Lori and said, "I'm sorry about the last bike ride. I'm sorry I scared Mary Lynne."

Lori smiled and said, "Mary Lynne likes you a lot, Andy. So do I."

It was as though her words went di-

rectly to his heart and then spread out
in a warm joy all over his body. It didn't
matter to him that the wind was wail-
ing outside or that he was cold and
uncomfortable sitting inside the lighthouse. It seemed to him that the best
thing in the world had just happened to
him. Without thinking, he leaned forward, put his arms around Lori and
kissed her on the mouth.

For one glorious moment, Lori
seemed to nestle into his arms and
return his kiss. He wanted that moment to last forever.

Then Lori drew back, pushed Andy
off the log, stood up, and asked him,
with a face as white as ash, "What do
you think you're doing?"

Andy jumped up beside her and
reached out to touch her arm. He said,
"Wait a minute, Lori. I want to talk to
you."

She pushed Andy away a second time
and ran out of the lighthouse into the
storm. Andy watched her run across
the beach, then he turned, kicked sand
over the fire, and ran after her. The day
was ruined. In fact, he'd probably ruined everything.

6

Lori ran through the storm just as fast as she could. Somehow, the crackling lightning and the thunder all around her seemed to be a natural accompaniment to her flight.

As she was running, she wasn't sure why she was so frightened. If anyone had asked her, she would have to admit that she wasn't really frightened of Andy. She knew him too well. But she wasn't thinking as she was running. All she was doing was feeling. She was feeling the cold air snap against her skin. She was feeling the darkness close in around her.

By the time she'd crossed the sand and gotten to her own bicycle, she was breathing in great huge gulps of air, and her heart was beating fast. It seemed terribly important to get to her bicycle before Andy got there. He was calling to her now, waving his hands and calling, "Lori. Lori. Wait for me."

She ignored him. Bending down, she struggled with trembling fingers to put on her shoes. It was difficult work to get her shoes on because her fingers were cold and stiff.

Andy was panting and out of breath when he reached her. He leaned over and touched her on the shoulder, saying, "Lori, I'm sorry. I'm sorry. I don't want to scare you away."

Lori jerked her shoulder away from him and snapped, "You couldn't scare me, Andy Johnson." As she said this, she stood up and swung her leg over her bicycle.

Andy said, "It's too wet to ride. Let's go to the Visitors' Center, and I'll call my mom."

Lori wanted with all her heart to refuse, but she knew it would be ridiculous to ride home in a storm like this. She thought about calling her own mother so she wouldn't have to ride with Andy; but her mother was at work, and though she would have come in an emergency, it would be difficult to explain. There was no way out of it. She would have to stay with Andy until they got home.

She nodded in agreement and jumped onto her bicycle. It felt awful trying to pedal through the deep rivulets of water that coursed down the sides of the path. Bicycling through sandy mud wasn't much fun.

Twice Lori turned to look to see if Andy was still behind her. She didn't really care whether he was with her or not. She was never going to speak to Andy again. Not if she could help it!

The Visitors' Center was closed, so they had to go all the way into town. It was a tough, unpleasant ride, and Lori felt as though she were struggling uphill all the way. When Andy took the lead, she let him.

Andy pointed to a large diner down the street. There was a big neon sign that said SAM'S SEAFOOD, and over that sign was a neon picture of a large swordfish.

Lori nodded, and they pedaled toward the parking lot. Soon they were standing in the entryway of the restaurant, letting some of the water drip down them onto the orange carpet.

A woman carrying menus came up to

them and asked in a worried voice, "Are you two all right?"

Andy spoke first. "We're fine. We just want to have something to eat while we wait for a ride."

"You look as though you'd been out in the storm forever," the woman said.

Lori didn't answer her but turned to Andy and asked, "You need a dime? You'd better call your mom."

Andy turned away from Lori and asked the woman, "Where are your telephones?"

"Right over there." The woman pointed, and Andy walked toward the hallway. She asked Lori, "You and your boyfriend walking in this?"

"Bicycling," Lori snapped. "And he's not my boyfriend."

"Brother?" the woman asked.

"No."

When Andy came back he said shortly, "Mom will be here in thirty minutes. We should have lunch. We never did eat our sandwiches." As Lori thought of the soggy sandwiches she'd left sitting on a rock inside the lighthouse, she wanted to cry. How had such a good beginning turned so awful?

Lori followed Andy to a booth by the window, and they both ordered hot tea and cheese sandwiches.

When the woman brought the sandwiches, she said brightly, "You two dried off a little bit, huh?"

Andy and Lori nodded and smiled at the woman, but they didn't nod or smile at each other. Lori ate her sandwich slowly and fought the tears that were behind her eyelids. She absolutely was not going to let Andy see her crying. She wasn't going to let Andy know that she was upset if she could help it. It was none of his business. Besides, he might think that he was important to her if she cried over him. Andy Johnson was not important to her. At least, not anymore. As far as she was concerned, once they got home from this miserable bike ride, she hoped she never saw him again as long as she lived.

By the time Mrs. Johnson had arrived with the station wagon, they were finished with their sandwiches and were sitting opposite one another, each studiously avoiding the other's eyes.

Lori reached into her pocket and pulled out a five-dollar bill. Andy said, "I'll pay for it."

Lori's eyes blazed as she snapped, "No, you won't. I'll pay for my own."

They walked out to the car where Mrs. Johnson waited for them.

"You two certainly picked a fine day for a bike ride, didn't you?" Mrs. Johnson said.

"Couldn't have been worse, could it?" Lori forced a laugh.

"Did you have any fun?" Ruth Johnson asked.

Lori felt her face flush with sudden embarrassment. She stammered, "Not much."

Andy, who was sitting in the back seat, chimed in, "It was pretty miserable."

Somehow they managed to endure the ride home. When they drove up to Lori's house, she turned and said, "Thanks for the ride, Ruth. I really appreciate it."

"Can't let my favorite kids drown like rats, can I?" she answered.

Lori opened the car door, and Andy opened his. She said to Andy, "I can get my own bike."

"I'll help you," Andy said.

They went around to the back of the station wagon and lifted her bicycle out and onto the ground. Lori turned to Andy and said, "Well, see you."

Andy said in a strained voice, "Lori, don't be like that."

"Like what?" Lori answered. "I'm not like anything." With that, she took her bicycle and wheeled it toward the back door of her apartment building. She tried not to think about the hurt look on Andy's face. It was best not to think about anything at all.

She spent the rest of the afternoon washing her hair, taking a hot bath, drinking tea, and reading books. As far as she was concerned, she was going to spend a lot of time by herself from now on. She would just have to forget about Andy. He was Melissa's boyfriend and had no business kissing her. She remembered how she had felt when Andy had kissed her and flushed with embarrassment again. She certainly hoped that he didn't think she had wanted him to kiss her. Had she been too slow pushing him away? Had he gotten the wrong idea? And then she remembered the hurt look on Andy's face. No, she'd certainly been definite enough. He understood that much at least.

The next couple of days, Lori did everything she possibly could to avoid Andy. When she saw him at school, she said hello very quickly and got out of his way. On Tuesday, he asked her if she wanted to go bowling that night, saying, "Some guys are going. I thought maybe you wanted to come along."

"No," Lori said. "I promised to pick up Mary Lynne after school."

Andy nodded his head and said, "Well, maybe later this week. Huh, Lori?"

Lori felt confused. How could she explain to Andy that things had changed between them? Somehow, that kiss had made things very different for her. She didn't feel the same way about Andy. But she wasn't sure exactly how she did feel. It was dumb to think of Andy as a boyfriend, and now she couldn't think of him as a friend either.

She sighed and said, "We'll see, Andy." Then, before he could ask or say anything else, she turned away from him.

Lori spent the afternoon with Mary Lynne, but she couldn't get Andy off her mind. She kept wondering what he was doing at that particular moment. She tried to ignore these thoughts and help Mary Lynne with her schoolwork. Finally, about five o'clock, she asked Mary Lynne if she'd had enough for today.

Mary Lynne nodded her head quickly and stacked her books in one corner. Then she looked at Lori and asked, "Can we go to Andy's?"

"Not today."

"Don't you like Andy anymore?" Mary Lynne asked.

Lori was startled. "I still like Andy," she said.

"Then why can't we go to visit?"

"He's busy," Lori said shortly.

Mary Lynne seemed to accept her answer, but Lori worried about what the little girl was really thinking. She hugged her and smoothed the hair off her forehead as she tried to explain. "Andy and I are still friends. But sometimes people change."

"My daddy changed. Then he went away," Mary Lynne said.

Lori held Mary Lynne tighter. She'd used the wrong words! She knew that Mary Lynne's father had deserted her. She didn't want Mary Lynne to think anything bad was happening between her and Andy. It would only make her more distrustful.

Lori said quickly, "Andy's not going to go away."

"It's okay," Mary Lynne said in a wistful voice. "You're my big sister. I don't need a big brother, too."

Lori frowned at the sky. Why did everything seem to make her feel guilty these days? She realized her anger toward Andy was long gone. Now all she felt was sadness and loss.

Lori wished there were someone she could talk to about her problems. There were only two people in the world she'd always been able to talk to, and they were both cut out of her life now. She couldn't talk to Andy's mother about this problem. And Andy was gone from her life forever.

At school, Lori made a point of avoiding Andy. Whenever she saw him, she said hello and rushed on to do something else. A couple of times, she saw him talking to Melissa in the school cafeteria, but most of the time he hung out with his friends Pat and Louis. Lori kept as busy as she could. She packed her own lunch and ate it in the library while she pretended to do research for her science project.

She tried not to think at all about the kiss they had shared on the beach; the feelings that the kiss had aroused seemed silly and exaggerated. It wasn't just the kiss that upset her. It was also the fact that she'd run away from Andy. What kind of a silly kid did he think she was? No sixteen-year-old girl runs away just because she's been kissed.

Lori decided it did absolutely no good to think about it. Their friendship was over, finished and done. Andy seemed to feel the same way because on Thursday when she passed him in the hall, he deliberately turned his head so he wouldn't have to speak to her.

That snub made her feel terrible. She never dreamed her friendship with Andy Johnson could end this way! It seemed so wrong and so sad.

She walked away from Andy, fighting

the tears that threatened to overflow her eyelids and spill onto her cheeks. But even as she was fighting back the tears, she was aware of other feelings. She was angry at Andy—terribly angry. She wanted to tell Andy that he had ruined everything. Why had he kissed her? Was he turning into one of those macho characters who had to make a pass at every girl just because she was a girl? Had he momentarily forgotten that Melissa was his girlfriend? These thoughts swirled round and round in Lori's head, but no matter how many times she tried to understand, things just seemed to get more complicated.

Lori felt even worse when her mother asked her, "Whatever's happened to Andy? I haven't seen him all week. You two used to be inseparable. Have you had a fight?"

"I guess he's busy," Lori said. When her mother waited to hear more, she remained stubbornly silent. She was not ready to share her feelings.

As Lori ran down the street toward the park, she tried to make her mind a blank. She was tired of thinking about Andy. She concentrated on running.

She ran past the gray-shingled houses, past the short black pine trees, down toward the beach where the boats were docked around the wharfs, past the seafood restaurants, past a boarded-up disco and the shell and souvenir shops and then on to the shopping center. She ran around the parking lot of the shopping center twice. As it was getting dark, she turned and ran back toward her home, retracing her steps.

When she got to her apartment, her mother looked up from setting the table and asked, "Where in the world have you been, Lori?"

"Running," Lori answered shortly, her shoulders heaving as she gasped for air. Sweat was streaming down her face and running in little rivulets down the back of her running suit. She worked her shoulders in a circular movement, feeling loose, happy, and relaxed for the first time since last Saturday. She smiled at her mother and added, "I think I ought to run two hours every night before dinner instead of one."

Her mother frowned. "You're skinny enough. An extra hour of running won't do you much good."

"Sure it will, Mom. Get me in shape for the baseball season," Lori answered, and she swung her leg over the back of the kitchen chair and sank down into the seat.

Her mother set the meat loaf on the table and said, "Lori, I wish you wouldn't sit down like that. And please remember to change clothes before supper. I want you to start acting like a normal teenage girl instead of doing that imitation of Willie Mays."

Lori laughed. She knew her mother was proud of her athletic prowess even though she was as unathletic as they came. She said, "Can't you think of any other baseball players except Willie Mays? He hasn't been around for twenty years, you know."

"He was good though," her mother said pleasantly. "Your father took me to see him once."

"Was that the only baseball game you ever saw?" Lori asked.

Her mother nodded her head and smiled. "It was my first date with your father. I was eighteen years old."

Lori felt a sudden pang of sadness. She couldn't imagine that her mother had ever been eighteen years old. Since her father had died when she was two, she couldn't imagine him at all. All she knew about him was in the photo album on the bookshelf and the stories her mother told.

She looked at her mother. Her mother's face looked tired. Little lines ran down from the side of her nose to her chin. She was almost forty years old. Lori felt a sudden stab of fear. What would she be like when she was forty years old? What would she be like as an adult?

Shaking her head to clear her brain of such thoughts, she reached across the table for the potatoes. "Ask for them," her mother said sharply. "I'll pass them to you."

"Sorry," Lori muttered as she put two potatoes onto her plate.

Her mother smiled. "I love to see you eat, Lori. You're such a healthy, happy youngster. You always were."

Lori frowned. She didn't like having her mother refer to her as a youngster. Then she laughed out loud at her own confusion. One minute she was terrified of growing older. The next minute she was angry because her mother called her a youngster. Didn't anything please her anymore?

While they were finishing dinner, her mother asked, "Why don't you call Andy and see what he's up to?"

"I don't care what he's up to," Lori answered.

"It seems to me if you two had a quarrel, it's about time to patch it up."

"We didn't quarrel," Lori said shortly.

Her mother said, "Good friends are worth keeping. Remember that."

Lori bit her lip and didn't answer. She couldn't think of anything to say except, "I'll do the dishes."

"Thank you," her mother said. Then she smiled and added, "Besides, I was going to the movies with Dorothy. I hope you don't mind."

"Have a good time," Lori said.

"Do you want to go with us?" her mother asked.

"No thanks."

"I don't know," her mother said. "This just isn't like you, Lori. You've been sitting home alone all week, and you look so sad. Are you sure you don't want to talk about what's going on?"

"I'm sure I don't want to talk about it, Mom," Lori answered.

Her mother stood beside her for a few minutes, watching her rinse the dishes. When Lori didn't say anything else, she shrugged her shoulders and turned and walked out of the kitchen. As she walked into the hallway the phone rang, and Lori's mother answered it.

She called out, "Lori, it's Andy," and went into her own bedroom, shutting the door behind her.

Lori's hands were shaking as she lifted the telephone receiver to her ear.

After she'd said hello, Andy said quickly, "Don't hang up, Lori. I want to talk to you."

"I'm here."

"I want to apologize for last Saturday. I don't know what got into me."

Lori felt her heart thumping as she tried to decide what to answer.

"I'd like us to go back to just being friends," Andy continued. "You know, just like the old days. I'm really sorry, Lori. I promise, nothing like that will happen again."

"I certainly hope not." Lori was pleased that her voice wasn't trembling even though her hands were.

"It was crazy," Andy said. "Sometimes I'm crazy. I guess maybe I'm just kind of girl-crazy right now or something. You know, it was all Melissa's fault. Honest, Lori. It had nothing to do with you."

"I don't want to hear about Melissa," Lori interrupted. "I don't care what you do with Melissa, but I'm supposed to be your friend."

"You are, Lori. You're the best friend I have. Honest to goodness, Lori, it'll never happen again. Please accept my apology."

"Don't apologize any more," Lori said. "I accept. I accept."

"Then we're friends again?" Andy asked.

Tears welled up behind her eyelids as she said, "We can try, Andy. But I don't know if it's going to work."

"It's going to work," Andy said. "Honest, Lori."

"Okay, Andy, if you say so," Lori said reluctantly. She could hear relief in Andy's sigh.

"Then it's all settled? We're friends again?"

"We're friends," Lori conceded.

"Then can I come over tonight?" Andy asked.

For one wild moment, Lori felt afraid.

What if she said yes and Andy tried to
kiss her again? She'd be in the house
alone. And then she reminded herself
that Andy wasn't interested in her.
He'd said it was Melissa who'd made
him crazy. It was Melissa he was interested in. Lori said, "What about Melissa?"

"What about her?" Andy asked.

"Don't you want to invite her, too?"

"Why would I invite Melissa?" Andy
sounded bewildered.

"But you just said it was Melissa you
were interested in," Lori said. "Was
that a lie?"

"No, no. Everything I told you was
the truth."

"Then if it's Melissa you're interested
in, I could call her up and invite her
over, too," Lori insisted.

Andy was silent for a moment. Then
he said quietly, "Thanks, Lori. I really
appreciate that, and maybe I'll take you
up on it sometime soon, but right now I
think it would be better if I talked to
Melissa privately. You know what I'm
saying?"

"Then are you sure you want to come
over here tonight?" Lori asked.

"Of course I'm sure. We could go

bowling or watch television or do anything you want."

"Anything?" Lori asked.

"Anything," Andy assured her.

"Well then. Tonight I'd like you to play chess with me again," Lori said. "I've read a book, and I think I'm better at it."

She knew that Andy hated to play chess with her because he was so good, and though she practiced a lot, she'd never really gotten the hang of the game. Usually, Andy made up some kind of excuse or tried to avoid playing with her, but today he didn't argue.

"Sure," he agreed halfheartedly.

Lori said, "Okay. Tonight we'll just spend the time together, and then maybe this weekend I'll have a party and invite Melissa."

There was another silence on the phone, and then Andy said, "Sure, Lori. Whatever you think."

"It'll be fun," Lori said. "I've been going to have a party for a long time. Now I've got a good excuse. I'll invite Pat and Louis and Melissa and maybe that new boy Tommy, the one who's supposed to be so good at baseball. It'll be a good chance to get to know him before the season starts, don't you think?"

"Whatever you say," Andy said.

"Well then. I think that we can even start planning for the party tonight—after I've beaten you at chess, that is."

"You'll never beat me," Andy said with assurance.

"We'll see," Lori said. "We'll see." Perhaps everything would work out after all. They could both forget that entirely unimportant kiss on the beach.

7

Lori's mother was so glad that Lori and Andy were friends again that she didn't even argue about having a back-to-school party. All she said was, "Remember that an apartment won't hold more than eight or ten kids."

It took Lori a little while to pare her list down to fourteen. She finally decided to have Melissa and her best friend, Betty Sue. She also invited two girls that she was friendly with in gym class. It turned out to be five girls and nine boys, since her friends were mostly boys on the baseball team, and none of them had girlfriends.

On the night of the party, Lori was pleasantly surprised when Melissa called and asked if she could come early to help. Lori agreed to have her come at five o'clock and help her make the sandwiches and dips for the party.

Melissa arrived wearing a beautiful pale pink cashmere sweater and white flannel slacks. Lori looked down at her own Levi's and cotton shirt in dismay as she said, "Oh, I didn't plan for this to be a dress-up party."

Melissa smiled sweetly and said, "Neither did I. That's why I wore slacks."

Lori felt embarrassed by her own casual appearance. She kept giving Melissa sidewise glances. How did Melissa get her hair to turn under that way? Did she set her hair on rollers or use a hot comb? Lori smiled ruefully as she thought about her own tousled head of curls. She'd spent more time than usual running her fingers through her head to get the curls to stand up, rather than lie flat around her face. And for makeup, she'd borrowed some of her mother's light coral lipstick.

Now, standing beside Melissa, she felt tall and awkward. No wonder all the boys were crazy about Melissa, she thought. Melissa was exactly the kind of girl that boys were supposed to like.

Yet Melissa was also the kind of girl that she never wanted to be.

She busied herself getting the plates of sandwiches ready and tried to think of things to talk to Melissa about. But Melissa's interest in sports was very limited, nor did she want to talk about school. The only topic that interested Melissa was boys. She ran through a whole list of boys that Lori had never even thought about. As she named each one, she demanded that Lori tell her whether she thought he was cute. Lori, feeling very silly about the whole conversation, tried to be as objective as she could in her evaluation of the boys. Melissa finally asked Lori for her opinion of Andy.

"Andy Johnson?" Lori asked.

"Yes. Don't you think he's darling?" Melissa asked.

"Andy?" Lori repeated. She didn't know exactly what to say. If she told Melissa that Andy was darling that might be worse than saying no. She was happy when the doorbell rang, and she could get out of answering the question.

Pat and Louis were at the door. Lori brought them into the kitchen and put them to work. Pat, who was a nonstop talker, seemed to be eating more sandwiches than he was making as he launched into a conversation about this year's chances for the football team. At last Lori was at ease. She could talk about sports knowledgeably. It was a lot more in her line to talk about the athletic ability of various players than how cute they were. Cuteness was nothing but opinion anyway.

Pat and Louis and she carried on a three-way conversation until the rest of the guests arrived. By the time the party had started, Lori had forgotten all her awkwardness with Melissa and was ready to have a good time.

She felt comfortable with so many of her old friends around and was glad that she'd made so many sandwiches, which were rapidly being devoured. She felt relaxed and cheerful because her guests seemed to be having a good time. At least, most of her guests were having fun. Melissa looked bored, and Lori wished she could think of some way to help her have fun, too. Andy wasn't even talking to Melissa.

About ten-thirty, Melissa jumped up from her chair and called out, "You know what's wrong with this party? Too much food and not enough exercise. Let's dance."

Lori raised her hands to indicate helplessness and said, "There really isn't any room. The apartment's too small."

"Oh, sure there is," Melissa said. "Come on Betty Sue, help me."

Lori watched with dismay as Melissa and her friends pushed all of the furniture back in the dining room and rolled up the rug so that they could dance. She felt funny that the idea had never even occurred to her, but she admitted that rolling back the rug made a perfectly good dance area. For the first time all evening, it occurred to Lori that there was something slightly peculiar about her guest list. Having only five girls at the party now seemed strange, especially when Melissa and the other girls asked Andy and three other boys to dance. Lori was left sitting, talking to the other five boys.

She tried not to let it bother her as the girls put on one record after another and traded boys, asking one boy after another to dance. Melissa asked Andy to dance every other time, and Lori didn't know what to think about that. There was no doubt about it. Melissa really liked Andy. Lori knew that she should be happy for him. Hadn't Andy just told her that he was crazy about Melissa?

She didn't understand why she should feel so annoyed, so she just tried to ignore her feelings and kept on laughing and talking to the other boys.

When Louis asked her to dance, she wanted to say no, but it seemed more difficult than saying yes. She let Louis lead her onto the small dance floor, and when he put his arm around her, she felt herself stiffen and all her muscles tensed.

Louis, who was an old friend, seemed not to notice how stiff and frightened she was as he tried to lead her around the dance floor. They didn't talk, partly because Lori was busy counting under her breath to make her steps keep time with the music. Finally, the beat of the music changed, and Louis let her go.

Without anyone holding her, Lori was a lot more at ease. She'd watched enough of the others to do a good imitation of their dancing style. It was more a matter of holding your shoulders and neck straight while you moved your hips and legs. The steps themselves were easy enough—just a sort of small hop from side to side. And then there was the trick of bending your knees and bobbing up and down as you twisted. That part was easier. Anything was easier than trying to follow someone who was holding onto you. No more slow dancing, Lori promised herself as she kept time to the beat of the music. Then the record was over, and Lori started back to the couch where a couple of boys were still talking about sports. As far as she was concerned, she never wanted to dance again. It was easier to sit with the guys and talk about the things that they were interested in.

To her surprise Louis put his arm around her waist as they walked back into the living room. He said in a low voice, "That was great, Lori. You're a good dancer."

"I am?" she asked.

He squeezed her waist and smiled, saying, "I knew you would be, you being so athletic and all. How about going out with me next weekend? We could go to the disco in Provincetown."

"Oh, I don't think so," Lori answered quickly.

Louis frowned and said, "I thought you and Andy broke up. He seems to spend a lot of time with Melissa these days."

"Andy was never my boyfriend," Lori said. "We're just best friends."

Louis grinned at her and squeezed her waist again as he said, "Well then, there's no reason why you can't go with me next Saturday night, is there?"

Lori was stumped for an answer, and so she opened her mouth and closed it without saying anything. She was surprised that Louis wanted to take her out. He always dated girls who were very sophisticated. In fact, his last girl had been a freshman in college. She liked Louis, but she wasn't sure they would have much in common.

At that point, Pat jumped off the couch and said, "How about me, Lori? Are you going to let me stay here and be a wallflower all night?"

She went back onto the dance floor with Pat and danced with him. At least that saved her from answering Louis right away. She wondered what Andy would think if she went out with Louis. Would he care? Of course not. Andy had Melissa, and she was a free agent. She could say yes to Louis if she wanted to. That is, if he'd really meant it. Lori glanced anxiously over at Louis. Was he really interested in her? It would be a first date for her, but she didn't have to tell him that. She might as well start with him. She would tell him yes.

Because she'd been so busy thinking about Louis, she'd been less self-conscious with Pat. By the time their dance was finished, she realized she was actually enjoying herself.

When Charlie asked her to dance, she managed to smile and say, "Sure," with her usual cheery enthusiasm.

From then on Lori danced every dance. The boys took turns asking her, and the party took on a different, more festive, air. Lori was surprised to discover that she enjoyed the excitement of having the boys laugh and tease each other about who got to dance with her next. Though she had never thought she would enjoy being chased by boys, she admitted to herself that it was kind of fun.

Melissa whispered to her as they went into the kitchen for more sandwiches, "I'm having a great time, Lori. It was smart of you to invite so many extra boys."

Lori flushed with anger at the idea that Melissa thought that she had intentionally invited twice as many boys just in order to get extra attention.

She was having a pretty good time at her party and had danced twice with every boy in the room except Andy. They hadn't even talked. But every time she looked for Andy, he was talking to Melissa.

Don't complain, she said to herself. After all, she had really arranged this party so that Andy and Melissa could get together. Now it was happening, so the party must be a success. Right? She forced herself to smile brightly and talk with Pat as they danced. She was trying not to notice how wrapped up Andy was with Melissa. Melissa was glowing with excitement. She smiled up at Andy and batted her long dark eyelashes at him. Lori wondered how Melissa could open her eyes so wide with all that junk on her lids. She compared her own plain, healthy looks to Melissa's carefully set golden curls. She wondered if Andy would like her better if she had carefully arranged golden curls. Stop thinking about Melissa and Andy! she told herself. If Andy wanted to be dumb enough to chase a phony like Melissa, it was his business.

By the time Lori had danced with each of the boys twice, she was tired of moving around in small circles in the limited space of the dining room. She felt that she preferred getting her exercise by running around the track or doing something else more energetic. But you could hardly suggest a fast run around the block to a bunch of kids who were having a party.

All in all, the party was a success, she decided. And she'd made her first real date with Louis for next Saturday night. That was an event—whether good or bad she wasn't sure. She did her best to act like Melissa and the other girls, flirting with the boys and trying to behave properly for the party setting.

She must have done a pretty good job of it, she decided, because a couple of the other guys seemed to be interested in her. Jim tried to drag her into the darkest corner of the living room, saying he wanted to talk to her. She followed him into the living room and sat on the small footstool that he pointed to. Then he kneeled beside her and took her hand in his. He ran his fingers over her hand as he said, "I know you must be upset about Andy, but there's really nothing to be upset about, Lori. You're too good for him."

Lori tried to jerk her hand away and said, "I don't know what you're talking about. Andy and I are just friends."

Jim smiled and held her hand more tightly as he said, "Of course I understand. It must be difficult for you after all these years, but things change. People grow apart."

"You sound like a bad movie, Jim, and I don't know what you're talking about," Lori said.

He pressed her hand between his as though he had captured a small bird, and he said softly, "I know what you and Andy have meant to each other. Andy has talked about you to me several times, and I know that you must be hurt to see him with Melissa, but life goes on. People change. I'm going to make it up to you, Lori. You'll see."

Lori jumped up off the stool and said angrily, "You're making up this big dramatic thing, and none of it is true. None of it at all."

Jim smiled a superior, slow, secretive smile. "You don't have to pretend with me, Lori. I know all about you two."

Lori felt the blood rush from her face, and her hands clenched and unclenched with anger. She was annoyed at Jim, and at the same time, she was angry at Andy. What had he said about her? Had he been talking to the boys all this time? Andy wouldn't do a thing like that, would he? Three different boys had said something to her this evening about her and Andy breaking up. They wouldn't all have said anything unless Andy had been talking about her. What had Andy been saying? Was he telling his friends that they had been a couple? It was hard to believe that Andy would do anything like that, but it made a kind of sense. Look at the way he was acting about Melissa!

She stared at Andy dancing with Melissa in the corner of the dining room.

His dark brown hair looked blue-black in the soft dining room light. His chin touched the top of Melissa's soft golden curls. Looking at them so together, Lori decided that Andy was as silly as Melissa. She couldn't stand Melissa Gaylord, and she couldn't stand Andy Johnson.

It took all of her energy not to go over to the dark corner where Andy and Melissa were and confront him. She wanted to break them apart and really give Andy a piece of her mind. But at the same time, another, more sensible part of her mind was saying, Hey Lori, cool it.

By the time her mother came in from visiting with her friends, Lori was close to tears. She was glad when her mother walked in the back door of the apartment and called out, "Party's over. One o'clock. Cleanup time. Lori, you'd better get some of your friends in here to clean up this mess." Lori quickly turned on the living room and dining room lights.

Melissa and Andy blinked in the bright light. Lori said in a sharp voice, "Andy, you'd better get in here and help me." She was pleased to see that he quickly dropped his hands from Melissa's waist and turned to come into the kitchen to help her clean up.

Some of the kids, including Melissa, claimed that one o'clock was their curfew and went home. Others stayed and helped Andy and Lori wash the dishes and clean up the kitchen. It was almost a quarter to two when Andy threw the tea towel over the rack and smiled at Lori. "You gave a great party," he said.

"You looked like you were having a good time," Lori said ironically.

"Sort of." Andy shrugged.

"Did you make a date with Melissa?"

"I'm going to see her next Saturday night," Andy said.

"Maybe we could double date," Lori suggested. "I have a date with Louis."

"A date?" Andy repeated, obviously shocked.

"Actually three guys asked me to go out with them. Louis was the first," she said coolly.

She didn't know what reaction she hoped for, but it wasn't the one she got. Andy's expression changed so fast she really wasn't sure what he thought. He turned abruptly to pick up his jacket from the back of the kitchen chair and said, "Well, see you, Lori. I've got to go home now." Lori watched in silence as he threw his jacket over his shoulders and walked rapidly out of the kitchen.

The front door slammed behind him.

8

When Andy called Lori the following Sunday and suggested that he go bike riding with Lori and Mary Lynne, Lori was surprised. Andy hadn't spoken to her since the party except to say hello at school. They hadn't really talked since he had slammed out of the house. It felt so good to hear from him that she agreed. After all, it would do Mary Lynne good, and why should she hold a grudge? They had known each other too long for that. Besides, she was not really sure what they had been fighting about. It seemed silly to make a big deal about nothing.

Light flakes of snow drifted down on the three of them as they pedaled furiously against the wind. Lori began to sing "Jingle Bells." Mary Lynne's high,

sweet, clear voice chimed in. Then
Andy added his bass.

By the time they got back to Lori's
apartment, their fingers were stiff with
cold and their faces numb from the
biting wind.

"Whoever heard of snow in October?"
Lori asked.

"It will be sunny tomorrow," Andy
promised as he parked his bicycle in the
entryway. "Do you want me to put yours
and Mary Lynne's downstairs?"

"Yes. I'll make some cocoa to warm
us up."

Mary Lynne and Lori went into the
kitchen, and Mary Lynne began stir-
ring a mixture of sugar and cocoa in the
bottom of a bowl. While Mary Lynne
stirred the milk, Lori found some frozen cake in the top part of the freezer.
She popped it into the small toaster-
oven on low heat to thaw it out enough
to serve it.

As they worked, Mary Lynne asked
Lori, "Do you like men?"

Lori laughed and said, "Some men.
Not all of them."

"I don't like men," Mary Lynne said.
"I'm scared of them."

Lori's heart began to beat with excitement as she realized that, for the first time, Mary Lynne was actually talking about some of her fears.

She knew that it was good for Mary Lynne to get some of those feelings out, but at the same time, she felt that she should say something that was reassuring. "Lots of times I'm scared of things, Mary Lynne," Lori said. "Sometimes I'm scared to try new things. Sometimes I'm scared of people that seem different, but I try not to say I don't like *all* of one thing. You know what I mean?"

When Mary Lynne was silent, she went on, "I think it's better to say, I don't like such-and-such man. Not I don't like men. For example, you like Andy, don't you?"

Mary Lynne lifted the spoon from the chocolate pan up to her lips and tasted the warming milk as she rolled her eyes around the kitchen and seemed to be considering Lori's statement. After a long silence, she sighed and said softly, "I guess so. I like Andy."

"You just haven't known very many men," Lori pointed out. "You lived with your aunt, and you don't have any men friends."

"Neither do you," Mary Lynne said.

"I guess you're right," Lori admitted. She remembered her date with Louis the week before. She'd been shy and found it hard to talk at first, but she'd had a pretty good time. Was she afraid of him? Not really, she decided. Louis had tried to kiss her a couple of times, and she'd drawn away from him. When it was clear that she wasn't going to be affectionate, he seemed to lose interest in her. When he didn't ask her out, she'd been mildly disappointed, but she really hadn't been heartbroken.

Lori took the cake out of the oven. By the time Andy came into the kitchen, the two girls were talking about bicycle riding next spring.

"My legs will be longer then," Mary Lynne said.

"We could drive to Provincetown in my folks' car," Andy volunteered. "Maybe next weekend."

"Oh, could we?" Mary Lynne's eyes lit up with anticipation and pleasure. She loved Provincetown, loved the crowded streets and the excitement.

Lori said, "That's a good idea." Then she remembered her date with Pat.

"But we have to get back early," Lori said. "I have to be home by four-thirty."

"Four-thirty?" Andy asked. "Why so early?"

"I have a date," Lori answered hesitantly.

"Well, I have a date, too, but dates don't usually start until seven or eight o'clock."

"You're right," Lori said. She didn't tell Andy she wanted to wash her hair and get ready. She was afraid that would sound silly.

There was a long silence, and Lori picked at the chocolate cake in front of her. She lifted a mouthful and said, "I think freezing and baking a cake a second time makes it taste bad."

"So do I," Andy said.

They both pushed away the cake and sat looking at their plates. Mary Lynne began kicking her foot at the table leg in a rhythmic one-two, one-two count. The silence seemed to drag on interminably with no sound at all except the dull thud of Mary Lynne's foot pounding against the table leg.

Lori snapped at her. "Stop that."

Mary Lynne looked up at her with

tear-filled eyes. "Why are you acting so funny?"

"I'm not acting funny," Lori replied quickly. "Get your coat. It's time for you to go home." Then she realized that her voice was harsh and that Mary Lynne would think that taking her home now was some kind of punishment. She looked at her watch and said, "Well, maybe not this minute, but pretty soon. We have to get you home. Your aunt will worry."

Mary Lynne looked at her empty cake plate in front of her and said in a low, soft voice, "No she won't. She never worries."

"Well, I have homework to do," Lori said quickly.

"Are you mad at me?" Mary Lynne asked. "Your voice sounds so funny." Lori flushed and pushed her chair away from the table. She grabbed up Mary Lynne's plate and took it to the sink to rinse it. "If you have a date Saturday and Andy does too, how come you don't go together?" Mary Lynne asked above the running water.

Lori dropped the plate in the sink. The plate cracked and split in half. She reached in to pick up the pieces of the plate and cut her finger. Looking at her cut finger, she was able to find a release for the feelings that were welling up inside her. She looked at her finger. "Oooh, it hurts." Tears came into her eyes as she ran cold water over the cut.

Andy jumped up, ran over to the sink, and snatched up her finger to examine it. "It's only a little scratch," he assured her.

Lori pulled her hand from him. "You think it's only a scratch because it didn't happen to you!"

Andy stepped back as though he'd been slapped.

Lori knew her reaction was out of proportion, but it was too late.

"Do you want to go to the hospital?" Mary Lynne asked fearfully.

Seeing Mary Lynne's concern put things back into perspective for Lori. She laughed and hugged the little girl as she said, "No. I want to go to the bathroom and get a Band-Aid. It's not that bad, honey." She bent to kiss the little girl and added, "I'm sorry I was such a baby."

"You're not, Andy is," Mary Lynne said.

"I'll get the Band-Aids," Andy said quickly. He didn't look at either of the girls as he walked out of the kitchen.

Lori sensed that she and Andy were as far apart as ever. And now she had even upset Mary Lynne by snapping at Andy. Even though the rest of the afternoon passed without incident, the feeling remained. She and Andy would never be close again.

On the surface Lori and Andy were as friendly as ever. They had lunch together, waited for each other after school, and did homework together. They didn't bring up any touchy subjects and weren't critical of each other.

Lori was careful not to say anything about Melissa. The two times when she saw Andy talking to Melissa in the halls, she ducked and turned the other way to avoid running into them.

Andy didn't say anything about Pat either. Lori wasn't sure exactly how she felt about going out with Pat, but in a way it was exciting to be dating a second time. It gave her something to think about besides Andy. During the week she planned what she would wear several times and finally settled on a pair of school slacks and a brand new sweater her mother had given her. The sweater was a soft rose color and went well with her navy peacoat and gray-and-white striped muffler. She was wearing them when Pat picked her up.

It was the coldest October she could remember. A light crust of snow covered the dark brown grass in front of her apartment building when Lori walked out the front door with Pat.

Pat asked, "I thought we would drive to Provincetown and go to the movies, if you want. Would that be all right?"

"Sure," Lori said.

"We could see a double feature if you want," Pat offered. "There are a couple of good comedies at the Palace."

"Fine," Lori said.

"Or we could go bowling," Pat said.

"That's great, too," Lori said.

By now they were sitting in Pat's father's car, and he reached over to turn the ignition, then dropped his hands back and turned and faced her. He said, "Tell me what you want to do, Lori."

"I don't care," Lori answered.

Pat groaned, rolled his eyes skyward, and said in mock despair, "That's the trouble with being a boy. I always have to make all the decisions. You're lucky, Lori."

Though Pat was joking, Lori had the idea that behind the joke he meant it. She said, "Let's go to the movies."

"Unless you'd rather go bowling?"

They both laughed, and Lori said, "Let's flip a coin. Heads, the movies, tails bowling."

Pat pulled a nickel out of his pocket and flipped it into the air. Lori caught it and slammed it onto the back of her other hand. She said, "The movies. That's good."

On the drive to the movie, Lori asked, "What do you think our chances of winning the basketball championship are this year?"

"Not so great," Pat admitted.

"That's too bad. I think the baseball team is going to do well this year."

"You going to play second base?" Pat asked.

Lori shrugged and answered, "I'm hoping they'll give me a chance in the field. I'm faster this year."

"How does it feel," Pat asked, "being the only girl on the team?"

"It feels all right," Lori answered

shortly. She always felt funny when people asked her that. They seemed to expect some kind of answer, but she didn't know what it was. How could she explain to them that being on the baseball team felt perfectly normal to her? She'd always expected to play ball in high school. Baseball was an important part of her life.

"You think you're good enough to be a pro?" Pat asked.

Lori laughed and said, "No. Of course not."

"But on a women's team?" Pat persisted.

Lori shrugged and tried to explain. "Baseball is about as important to me as basketball is to you. People expect it to be very special because I'm female, but it's just a part of my life. I take it as something I do in high school. I don't have to turn it into a professional career or anything. If I were good enough maybe, but I'm just one more kid on a high school team as far as I can see."

Pat grinned as he said, "You're a lot prettier than the other kids on the team."

Lori laughed, pleased by the compliment, and they continued talking easily and freely about high school. By the time they reached the theater, Lori realized she was having fun. It was a lot like being out with Andy. After all, she was accustomed to the company of boys. Just because this was a date didn't mean she had to be miserable, she decided.

When they went into the theater, Pat bought her popcorn and said, "Do you want to sit up front or in the back?"

Instead of saying it didn't matter, Lori said firmly, "In the middle."

Pat found seats right in the middle of the theater. Lori enjoyed the first movie very much. It was a mixture of comedy and western, and she had always loved westerns. What she liked especially about this movie was that one of the cowboys was a woman. It was always more fun for Lori to see an action movie where the women did more than stand on the doorstep and wave good-bye. She thought she would tell Pat about that when the movie was over. It would give them something to talk about on the way home from the theater.

During the second feature, Pat held Lori's hand. She was a little surprised when he reached over, took it out of her

lap, and placed it on the armrest between the two seats. She would have
been happier to have her hand free, but
she didn't want to make a big deal out of
it. Hand holding was a normal part of
dating, she supposed.

The second movie seemed kind of
silly to her, and she was distracted by
Pat, who kept pressing her hand. She
found herself losing interest in the
movie and casting sidelong glances at
him, wondering what he was thinking.
Was he holding her hand because he
liked her or just because that's what
you did with a girl that you took out on a
date? What did Pat really think about
her? And had he been serious when he
said that he thought she was Andy's
girlfriend?

The thought of Andy made her uncomfortable, and she shifted her body
weight, moved in the movie seat, and
took her hand away from Pat.

He took it again as they were going
out of the theater. They walked across
the lobby holding hands as though they
had been sweethearts for a long time.

Lori was only mildly surprised when
she saw Andy and Melissa standing by
the popcorn machine. Her first reaction

was that she wanted to jerk her hand away from Pat. Andy would think she was silly and might tease her later. Then she realized that Andy no longer teased her about things like that. Besides, Andy was also out on a date, standing with his girlfriend beside him. No. They would not tease each other about this.

"I thought you guys were going to the party at Bev's house," Pat said.

Melissa frowned. "Andy decided he had to see these movies, so here we are." Her laughter trilled across the conversation and died. No one else seemed to find anything funny about Andy changing his mind.

Andy turned to Lori. "Did you like the movies?"

Lori nodded and said, "I liked the first one. I always like it when the women get to do something instead of stand around looking pretty and waving goodbye."

Andy nodded, taking this as a normal reaction, but Melissa seemed to think that Lori had been making a joke. She laughed once again. This time her laughter seemed higher and more nervous than before.

"How about a pizza?" Andy asked. Though the question was general, Lori could feel his intense blue stare on her. She accepted before the others had even a chance to answer, and the four of them turned and walked out of the movie lobby to the next-door pizza parlor. After much consultation they all settled on ordering a large with everything on it—the Supreme Deluxe.

"Pat was telling me that he thinks we may have a hard time beating Stanford High in the basketball game tomorrow," Lori remarked as they waited for their order.

"We'll have a hard time looking decent, let alone beating them. Still, if Tommy Bickford comes through the way he's been looking in practice, we might make some points," Andy answered.

"Really?" Pat asked. "Bickford's that good?"

"Getting good," Andy answered. "I watched him work out yesterday with the team. The coach made a mistake not putting him in at the beginning of the season."

Melissa yawned and put her hands over her mouth. Lori realized that her fingers were painted the same color as her pale pink lipstick. Lori wondered what it would be like to be a girl like that. Did she ever think about anything except how she looked and boys?

Lori was having a good time. Pat seemed to be having fun, too, and cracked a lot of jokes. Dating wasn't difficult when you got started, Lori decided. By the time the pizza was gone, she, Pat, and Andy had dissected the baseball, football, and track teams.

Melissa stood up and said in a bored voice, "I think we'd better go before you start on next year."

Lori realized they had spent the last forty-five minutes talking about something that Melissa knew absolutely nothing about. She turned to her and asked, "I'll bet you're excited about being a cheerleader, aren't you?"

Melissa's blue eyes flared. "We can't all be baseball stars; some of us have to be stuck on the porch waving goodbye."

Lori gasped. *Melissa's jealous of me*, she suddenly realized. How could a girl as pretty and popular as Melissa ever be jealous of her?

She reached out and put her hand on

Melissa's arm as she said, "I think it's wonderful to be a cheerleader. I would have been one if I hadn't been so tall."

Melissa shrugged off her hand and turned away. Is she really crying? Lori asked herself. And then she decided that was impossible.

"Will I see you tomorrow, Lori?" Andy asked when they were outside.

Lori nodded. "Call me around ten."

Andy turned and followed Melissa down the street.

Pat said in a tight voice, "I thought you said you weren't dating Andy anymore."

"I've never dated Andy," Lori said. "He dates Melissa."

"Then what are you going to do at ten o'clock tomorrow morning?" Pat demanded.

Lori laughed as she answered, "Oh, we might go down to the beach and pick up some driftwood. We've got a bunch of driftwood down in Andy's basement that we're thinking of trying to sell to tourists next summer."

"That's a date," Pat said.

Lori laughed and shook her head, placing her hand on Pat's arm in the same impulsive gesture that she had just made to Melissa. "It's not a date when it's with Andy. Andy and I are just friends."

Pat looked unconvinced but didn't say anything else. Lori asked him, "Will you make the county All-Stars this season?"

Pat began talking about football, and they didn't mention Andy or Melissa anymore that evening. On the way home from Provincetown, they talked about many things—mostly sports—but also about their plans after high school.

Pat wanted to go to college in Boston and major in history, but his folks were sure he should get into computers or engineering.

Lori told Pat that she knew she was very fortunate because her mother had never quarreled with her ambition to be a physical education teacher.

"Can you get jobs in phys ed when you finish?" Pat asked. "That's all my folks ever ask me. Can I get a job?"

"Oh yes. By the time I get out of school, there'll be a shortage," Lori assured him. And she realized that she was really a very lucky person to be so definite about what she wanted to do when she got out of school. It was nice to have a clear-cut, sensible future in front of her, Lori thought. All in all, going out with Pat had made her feel very good about herself.

As they drove up in front of her apartment, Lori decided that she liked dating very much. Pat killed the motor of the car and leaned forward to put his arm around her. Instead of pulling away, Lori let him circle her shoulders and pull her slightly toward him. When he bent his head to kiss her, she turned her lips up expectantly and returned his kiss. As she felt the pressure of his lips, she waited for some reaction. Where were the ringing bells, the electric thrills, the chills and fevers that she always saw in the movies? No, kissing Pat was not very thrilling.

As she pulled away, a car drove by. She was pretty sure it had been Andy, and she felt slightly excited by the possibility that Andy had seen her kissing Pat. She smiled at her date and said, "I had a nice time," then opened the car door. Kissing was probably something you had to practice before you enjoyed it, she reflected.

"I had a good time too, Lori," Pat

said. "Would you like to go out again next week?"

"I'd like to go out with you again, Pat, but I have a date." She hoped that Pat wouldn't ask who because she hadn't decided yet. All she knew was that she was going to start dating as many boys as she could. It was better than sitting around worrying about Andy.

9

Andy drove Melissa home very quickly. When they got to her front door, she turned to him with her face tipped up in a gesture that showed that she was ready to be kissed. Andy leaned over, brushed his lips briefly against hers, managed a tight smile, and said, "I'll see you soon, Melissa. Good night."

Melissa's big blue eyes seemed to fill with a satiny, glossy surface. For one wild moment, Andy wondered if she were going to cry. He hated to see girls cry. He leaned over and opened the car door for her. "Don't call me anymore, Andy, if you don't want to be with me," she said in a tight little voice.

"I don't know what you're so upset about," Andy answered. "All I did was talk about sports."

"All you did was flirt with Lori," Melissa retaliated quickly.

Andy laughed at that idea and said, "That's silly, Melissa. Lori didn't even look at me all evening. She was busy talking to Pat."

Melissa shook her head and said sadly, "If you can't be nice to me, just don't call me anymore. Okay?"

Andy grabbed Melissa's hand in his and squeezed it. "Melissa, I like you a lot. I really do. I'm not interested in Lori the way you think. I'm just not feeling so great this evening. Look, I'll call you next week. Okay?"

Melissa shrugged her slim shoulders and said, "I can't tell you what I'll be doing next week. I'll probably be busy."

Andy watched Melissa walk up to her front door with his hands clenched on the steering wheel. He was annoyed with himself for telling Melissa lies. But most of all, he was angry at Lori. Why did she have to flirt with Pat anyway? He thought that Lori was a better person than that. She'd really seemed to enjoy being with Pat, laughing at his crummy jokes.

He could see Lori's dimple in the side of her cheek every time she laughed at some joke Pat made. He saw her soft brown, curly hair shining in the dim light of the pizza parlor.

He started the ignition and drove away from Melissa's, promising himself he'd concentrate on other things.

It was an accident that he happened to drive by just as Lori had been kissing Pat good night. He was so angry he didn't even remember driving home and getting into bed.

His anger seemed to be even greater the next morning as he crunched on his breakfast cereal. His mother asked, "What's wrong? Didn't you have a good time?"

"Not very."

"I don't know why you keep dating that girl if you don't like her."

"I like her."

"No you don't! What are you doing anyway? Dating a girl you have nothing in common with while poor Lori sits at home!"

"Poor Lori!" Andy exploded. "Why do you and Tim both jump to conclusions? You both are so certain you know why I'm doing what I'm doing."

"Why are you dating Melissa?"

"For my own reasons," Andy answered.

"Such as?"

"Mom, I wish you'd lay off me." Why was everyone trying to run his life? He went over to the kitchen sink, rinsed off his bowl and glass, and left the room. There was no sense in trying to explain anything to anyone. Besides, he had to call Lori. It was for her own good! Someone had to tell her how silly she had been about Pat. Though he had made a date to see her at ten, he knew she was already up. It was seven, and Lori always got up at six. He even felt virtuous as he dialed her number.

"Hi, Andy. What's up?" Lori's voice was drugged with sleep.

"I wanted to talk to you about last night," Andy began and cleared his throat.

"Can't it wait?"

"No. I've been thinking that I have to tell you some things for your own good."

"What things, Andy?" Lori's voice sounded wary.

"I watched the way you were with Pat last night . . ."

"How was I?"

"Well, you were laughing, and you were silly, and you shouldn't be like that, Lori."

"Be like what?"

"You just shouldn't be so silly, you know. I mean like you seemed to think everything he said was funny. You kept laughing at his jokes."

"Pat makes funny jokes, Andy." This time Lori's voice was soft. If it had been some other girl, Andy might have thought that she was afraid, but he knew Lori very well. She was getting ready to tell him off. She always came on like some old John Wayne movie. She'd get very quiet and then, Pow!— she'd let him have it.

"Now don't get mad, Lori. What I'm telling you, I'm telling you for your own good. You were just really silly last night, and you looked dumb kissing him."

"Pat thought I looked just fine," Lori said, "and you know what, Andy? I didn't look nearly as dumb as that girl you were with. And you had no business spying on me. Besides, Melissa always laughs at your dumb jokes."

"That's different," Andy said. "We're

not talking about Melissa. We're talking about you."

"Correction," Lori said quickly. "We *were* talking about me. The conversation is over."

"I've got to tell you what I think. After all, we're good friends."

"That's the second time you've been wrong in two minutes," Lori said. "We were good friends. Not anymore. I need friends I can count on."

"Like Pat?" he asked. When Lori didn't answer, Andy said awkwardly, "Well . . . I'll see you at ten."

"No," Lori said. "I don't think so." Then she hung up the phone.

Andy spent most of Sunday talking to himself about how dumb he had been. By the time Sunday night came along, he'd called Lori's house three times to apologize. But each time Lori had been out. Andy didn't know whether she was refusing to talk to him or was really out. What was worse, he didn't know which would be better. If she wasn't speaking to him that would be one thing, but what if she were out with Pat again?

The next day at school Andy saw Lori

walking down the hall between Louis and Sammy. He stepped out of the hallway and said tensely, "Lori, I want to talk to you."

Lori turned her head slowly. "I'll talk to you later, Andy. I'm on my way to class now," she said. The bell for the first class rang. He saw her two other times in the hallway, but each time she pretended she didn't see him.

At lunchtime, Andy saw Lori with a group of kids on the other side of the room. She was clearly flirting with one of the senior boys. She seemed to be the most attractive girl he'd ever seen. No matter how difficult it was, he made up his mind that he would continue to pursue her. Lori was worth whatever trouble or pain she cost him.

He caught up with her again after school as she was walking down the steps with a group of boys. This time Andy was determined to make her talk to him if it was the last thing he did.

He called out in a clear voice, "Lori, you promised you'd talk to me. I'm waiting."

Lori stopped. She put her hand on Joe Brown's shoulder and said, "I'll be ready at seven, okay?"

Joe nodded, and he and the two other guys turned and walked down the stairs, leaving Lori alone to confront Andy.

Andy stepped closer, but before he could open his mouth, Lori said, "Andy, I suppose you want to get me to say that we're going to be friends all over again. But not this time. This time, I think we should just stay away from each other for a while. Every time we get together, we fight." Lori stopped and frowned at the cement steps beneath her feet. She added in a gentler voice, "Things just aren't working out for us anymore."

"The reason things aren't working is that you're always with other guys," Andy protested. He kept his voice low and carefully controlled. If he could keep from getting angry, maybe he would be able to make Lori understand that she was part of the problem. "This morning you were talking to Pat. At lunch you were with Joe, and now you're going to see him tonight. Think about what's happening to you, Lori."

Lori continued to look at the steps beneath her feet.

Andy's voice grew stronger and more persuasive as he went on, "You used to be the most sensible person I knew. Now you're acting like a silly kid."

Lori shook her head and said seriously, "I'm growing up, Andy, and part of growing up is learning how to get along with lots of people, not just one."

"But you're flirting with those guys," Andy said. "You never used to flirt."

"Am I flirting?" Lori smiled. Andy thought how beautiful her face looked in the afternoon sunlight. He'd never noticed it before but it seemed as though Lori's eyes weren't really blue at all. They were more of a deep purple color.

As he looked at her, he wanted to reach out and pull her close to him and kiss her. But it would only drive her farther away. Lori seemed to be interested in every boy in the school except him.

He decided to try a different tack. "What if I gave up Melissa?" he suggested. "And you gave up Joe? Then we'd be back where we were. We'd be even. We don't ever have to date anyone else, Lori. We could just be friends."

Lori shook her head, saying, "You're

missing the point. I don't want to give up dating Joe or anyone else. I'm going to date just as many boys as I can."

"Is that why you're flirting with everyone? So you can get a million dates?"

"I wasn't aware that I was flirting," Lori said coldly. "All I did was let them know I was interested in going out with them."

"And you're going to go out with someone else besides Joe?" Andy asked.

"I have four dates this week," she said smugly.

"Four dates," Andy repeated, dazed.

Nodding her head and smiling, she continued. "Yes. I'm going out with Joe tonight, and Louis asked me out again for Saturday. Pat on Friday, and guess who asked me to go to the football game?"

"I can't imagine," Andy said drily.

"Bud Allen."

"Bud Allen's dating Sally," Andy said.

Lori shook her head. "Not anymore. At least they're not dating steady. He wants to play the field, too."

"Play the field," Andy repeated, shaking his head in dismay. "Two weeks ago when you said 'play the field,' you would have meant baseball."

Lori laughed merrily and said, "I know, Andy, but I'm having fun." Then her blue eyes sobered up, and she turned to him, saying in a quiet voice, "Maybe we can be friends again sometime, Andy, but it will have to be different. You know, you made me very angry yesterday."

"And you made me angry," Andy retorted.

They stood, staring at each other on the school steps. Finally, Lori turned away, leaving Andy, his hands in his pockets, watching her slowly descend the steps, walk down the street, and around the corner. It occurred to him that if he and Lori had not known each other for so many years, they would still be speaking now. She might even have found him as attractive as Joe, Louis, or Bud. For the first time, he regretted all their good times growing up together. If he had not known her so well, she would have looked at him in a different light. She might even have considered dating him. But he was not even sure of that.

10

Lori had a wonderful time with Joe. They went bowling and then across town to the shooting gallery. She beat him unmercifully.

Later, on the ride home, she tried to give him the money he'd spent on the shooting gallery back, saying, "You shouldn't spend that kind of money on me."

But Joe laughed. "You're not like other girls, Lori. You're special. You're lots of fun to be with, and you're pretty, too."

Lori blushed with pleasure. She hadn't spent much time in her life thinking about how she looked, but lately a lot of people had been telling her how pretty she was. She had to admit she liked hearing it.

She liked Joe. But riding along beside

him in the car, she realized that she could never really be interested in him. He just wasn't her style. He was too quiet and too serious to suit her.

By the time they started home, she was exhausted from trying to keep the conversation going. If it had been Andy, she found herself thinking, there wouldn't have been this strained feeling every time silence fell. But being with Andy wasn't like being out on a date, Lori reminded herself. She couldn't expect other boys to treat her the same way that Andy did.

The thought of Andy made her sad. What had really happened between them? Maybe since he was involved with Melissa, there was no room for her in his life. Then she reminded herself that she had been responsible for their last quarrel. She didn't want to think about all that now. It was all too confusing. She forced herself to make small talk with Joe and pretended that she was very amused by his jokes. By the time she and Joe had reached her front door, her jaws ached from false laughter. I'm twittering like a canary, she thought. Just like Melissa. It's not really the way I feel at all.

She didn't feel very good about herself as she walked into her apartment. She felt as though she had become a different person. No matter what Joe said about her being pretty and nice, she felt dishonest. Why was it that everyone was saying nice things about her these days and she was feeling worse about herself?

When Sammy called and asked her out, Lori said yes though she was a little nervous about making the date. She didn't know Sammy very well, and he had a reputation. But he was good-looking, and she didn't want to say no. She told her mother she would be going out with him Thursday.

Her mother raised her eyebrows and said, "Another date? Don't you think you're overdoing it?"

"I'll be in early," Lori promised.

"I'd hate to see you turn into a social butterfly," her mother said.

Lori laughed and said, "Other mothers worry when their girls don't have boyfriends. Are you going to worry now that I've got some?"

"I'm not going to worry about you, ever," her mother answered gravely. "I know you're going to be all right. But

I wonder if two dates in one week won't be too many. After all, you're in school."

"I'll be in by ten-thirty," she promised.

"I'll have to be in by ten-thirty," she told Sammy when he came to pick her up.

Sammy looked disappointed. "I thought we'd drive over to visit my cousin in Boston," he protested.

"Boston?" Lori exclaimed.

"No, it's not really Boston. It's in the outskirts, and it just takes about an hour to get there."

Lori looked at her watch. It was seven-thirty now. If it took an hour each way that would leave an hour to visit. She said, "I'm sorry, but I guess it won't really work, will it?"

"No," Sammy agreed. "So what do you want to do? Want to drive out to the lake and make out?"

Lori stepped back in amazement. Was this the way Sammy thought he was supposed to act on a date? She was so taken aback by his question that she merely shook her head in reply.

He laughed too loudly and said, "I

was afraid the answer would be no. How about if we drive over and see Bud?"

"I have a date with Bud Saturday night," Lori said.

"So what?" Sammy asked. "Do him good to see you out with someone else. Let him eat his heart out."

"I don't think it's such a great idea," Lori said. Now she understood why Sammy had been so eager to date her. It was because she had become so popular. She was even more convinced of this when Sammy's next suggestion for their evening turned out to be visiting another friend of his on the baseball team.

As they drove to Charlie's house, she promised herself that she would never go out with Sammy again. If he couldn't think of anything more interesting to do than visit his friends, then why should she bother? She'd rather sit home alone.

Her evening turned out even worse than she had anticipated. Sammy and Charlie selected an old movie about destroyers to watch on television. Not only had Lori already seen it, but she hadn't like it the first time. By the time the tenth commercial break came along, she was yawning and looking at her watch every few minutes. When the movie was over, Lori jumped up and said, "I've got to get home now. It's almost ten-thirty."

On the way home Sammy said nothing until they pulled up to her door. Then he made a lunge at her, pinned her against the car seat, and gave her an awkward kiss.

She ducked out from under his arm, opened the car door, said, "See you," and practically ran into the house. Once inside the door she burst out laughing as she wiped the kiss off her lips. Poor Sammy! He had a lot to learn about girls, and she didn't intend to give him a chance to practice on her again.

It was with some nervousness that Lori went out on her third date that week. Richard was shy and dull. She treated him as gently as she could, suggesting that they go to the early movie. She insisted that she had to get home right after the movie. When he had driven her to her door, she leaned over, brushed her lips against his cheek, and said, "I had a nice time. Thanks for asking me."

Then he timidly asked, "May I call you again soon?"

She said evasively, "My mother doesn't like me to go out on dates too often, but we could do something together one of these days."

She was getting adept at letting boys down easily. The last couple of weeks had been a real social whirl. Since she'd started dating, it seemed as though a lot of boys in school were interested in her. It was almost as though she were a new girl in town. Although she was flattered by the attention, Lori had to admit to herself that she was beginning to find the whole thing boring. Dating was sometimes dull. Sure, it was fun to have a boy come to the door and tell you you looked pretty, but it wasn't much fun to have the rest of the conversation be stilted and phony.

By the time Bud picked her up on Saturday for the party, she felt as though she were the social butterfly of Orleans. When they got to the party, Bud went over to talk to some of his friends. In the old days, Lori would have politely gone with him, but to-night she didn't feel like it.

She stood in the corner for a while, looking at the other kids wander around. Most of the girls were dressed up in high-heeled shoes and fancy dresses. A few of them had obviously spent some time experimenting with makeup. There were two or three other girls who were wearing designer jeans and high-heeled shoes.

Lori decided that her dark blue slacks and blue-and-white striped sweater was probably the plainest outfit in the room. That made her feel dull and uncomfortable, and she wished Bud would come back and rescue her. Then she laughed at herself. Up until two weeks ago, she would have naturally expected to be on the sidelines. It was only since she'd blossomed and come to expect a lot of attention from boys that she was conscious of being alone.

She leaned against the wall with her hands in her pockets, one shoulder touching the wall, and looked around the scene with interest. Once she relaxed, Lori enjoyed watching the laughing, chattering nonsense that was going on around her. She was happy enough to hear snatches of conversation as people walked by her.

By the time Bud came back, Lori was having a great time. "I guess I'm really happier being an onlooker than anything else. You know, just being myself," she told Bud.

"How about a dance?" Bud asked.

"In a little while," Lori said. "Right now, let's just listen to the music." She hoped she wouldn't see Andy. She wanted to forget all about him.

When she finally saw him dancing across the floor with Melissa, she asked herself, What does he see in that silly girl? She's everything I never wanted to be. How could Andy have been friends with me all these years and then choose a girl like that? Thinking these things made Lori's detached enjoyment disintegrate into sadness.

In order to stay in the shadows and avoid their attention, she pretended to be much more interested in Bud's stories than she was. By the end of the evening, Bud was glowing with pleasure because Lori had been such an attentive audience. He related the whole story of his summer camping trip to Canada: from the day they first packed the car, all the way through the fish they'd caught, the kind of bait they'd used, the time they saw the grizzly bear, and now they'd watched geese fly south as they drove home to the Cape.

Lori stood with her hands in her pockets, leaning against the wall, her eyes glazed, staring up at Bud with a frozen smile. From time to time she heard herself falsely saying, "Is that so? Oh, that's so interesting, and then what?"

Bud, mesmerized by his own voice, went on and on. Lori was able to avoid talking with Andy and Melissa that night, but she wondered if it was worth the price she had to pay. When Bud took her home, she practically jumped out of the car and ran into her house.

Her mother was sitting in the living room watching an old movie on television. She called out, "Hi, Lori. Did you have a nice time?"

"Fine," Lori answered shortly and ran up the stairs to her bedroom. Once inside her bedroom, she did a series of exercises to loosen up her body. She could feel the tension in her shoulders and neck, and she hated feeling this uptight and anxious.

When she went to bed, she couldn't go to sleep. She lay staring at the dark ceiling, going over the events of the last few weeks in her mind. Finally, at three o'clock in the morning, she made her decisions. One—she was not going to go out with anyone she didn't like. Two—she was never going to worry about being popular. Three—she was never going to pretend to be interested in something she wasn't interested in. Four—when she did go out with a guy, she wasn't going to talk just nonsense. Five—of all the boys she knew, she still liked Andy the best.

Lori found she was relieved to be giving up the role of socialite. Let girls like Melissa compete in the popularity contest. She was going to be herself, she told herself as she drifted off to sleep.

11

Andy was proud of himself. He had managed to ignore Lori at the party. Somehow, it seemed like a real victory to have danced by her so many times and never once acknowledged her presence.

When he had awakened the next morning, his first thought was of Lori, dark-haired, lovely Lori, standing in the shadows. He remembered how her long slim neck had bent forward to hear what Bud was saying. He remembered, and it hurt him to remember it, how her lips had turned up in a slow, pleasant smile as she listened to Bud talking.

Again and again he'd danced Melissa by the corner where Lori stood in the half-light. Each time he'd wondered what it was that Bud could have been saying. What was so interesting? Dancing close to Lori was irresistible, like biting at a torn fingernail. It pained him, but he couldn't leave her alone.

Although his first thoughts were of Lori, his second thoughts were of Melissa. How was he going to tell her no? When she'd asked him to go to the Halloween party the next weekend, he'd said, "I'll talk to you about it tomorrow."

This was tomorrow, and he was going to have to find the words to tell her that he didn't want to see her anymore. His mother was right. It just wasn't fair to her to keep on dating her.

Andy jumped up out of bed, went over to the mirror over his dresser, and looked at his reflection. It was the same brown-haired, clean-cut, not too good, not too bad face that he'd always had. What had he really done? Nothing that awful! So what if he'd taken out a girl that he wasn't crazy about? How did that hurt anyone? Did it hurt Melissa? She would go out with lots of guys by the time she was twenty-five. So what was wrong if he wasn't her Prince Charming?

* * *

Later that day, Tim called him and asked him to come to supper that evening. "Alone?" Andy asked.

"Alone," Tim said. Then he added apologetically, "Patricia wants to talk to you."

Andy had a horrible feeling that Patricia was going to bawl him out for being so mean to her cousin, but there didn't seem to be any sensible way to turn the invitation down.

Sure enough, about ten minutes after he got to Tim's house, Patricia said, "I invited Melissa to come over later. She wants to talk to you."

Andy waited for Patricia to continue, but she quickly went on to another subject. "Your mother wants me to join her yoga class," Patricia said. Then she laughed. "Your mother is quite a woman."

At that moment, Melissa knocked on the door. When Patricia led her into the living room, she said, "Here's Melissa, who suggested that we invite you. But next time, Andy, I hope you'll get together on your own."

Andy didn't bother to reply to Patricia. He was too busy trying to think of things he wanted to say to Melissa.

Finally, he decided it would be much easier to talk if they were alone, so he said, "Melissa, let's take a walk."

Melissa, who didn't even have her coat off, smiled and said, "Sure, Andy." Then she looked at Tim and Patricia and smiled as if to say that she and Andy wanted to be alone as much as possible. Andy wondered what she had told them about their relationship.

Once they were outside, Andy said, "I'll take you to the dance, but that's the last time we'll go out together." He thought his words sounded rude, but he didn't know how else to get his point across to Melissa.

"I knew you would," Melissa answered quickly. "I already have my costume, and yours will be easy for me to make."

"You don't have to make me a costume," Andy protested, feeling guilty.

"I'm going as Juliet," Melissa rattled on happily. "I have my costume from last year's play. You probably remember it. The dress is yellow, and it has a black velvet vest. And I have this darling little cap with seed pearls all over it. It was my mother's wedding cap, and she's letting me wear it again. And my aunt Sylvia is buying me new dance slippers in yellow. I loved being Juliet, and it's a pretty costume."

She waited for Andy to say something, but he was silent. She went on, "Jim played Romeo last year, but he threw his costume away. I already asked him. Do you have any old pants we could cut off? No, never mind; yours would be too tight. Maybe I can find something in one of the thrift shops."

"I'm not going as Romeo," Andy said quickly. "Maybe I'll . . . I'll go as a pirate or something."

"You have to go as Romeo," Melissa said. "Otherwise I'll look silly. How will anyone know I'm Juliet if you're not Romeo? Don't worry about it. I'll work it all out with my mother. I'll bring you the costume Saturday afternoon."

"Melissa, I'm not going as Romeo," Andy repeated. "I'd just feel silly."

"You'll get over it," Melissa said quickly. "'By for now." She skipped off before he could even protest.

Andy did not see Melissa again until the following Thursday. She had not come to school the earlier part of the week, and when he called her house, her mother said that her cold was too bad for her to come to the telephone.

"Well then, can I come over?" Andy asked.

"No, Melissa won't be able to talk to you this evening," her mother said. "She said if you called to tell you she'd see you on Saturday."

A sudden suspicion hit Andy. Was it possible that Melissa was going to stay out of school all week just so he wouldn't have a chance to back out of the costume ball? No, that wasn't the sort of thing that a sweet girl like Melissa would do. Was it?

He called again on Wednesday, and this time he said, "Tell Melissa that if she doesn't come to the phone, I'm coming over there. I've got to talk to her."

But again, Melissa's mother was adamant. This time she said, "You can't come over. We're on our way to the doctor. Then Melissa will have to go home and go to bed. She'll see you in school tomorrow."

Andy had no choice but to hang up. He was more than a little suspicious now, but there wasn't anything he could do about it.

When he saw Melissa at school on Thursday, he called to her and waved. She pretended that she didn't see him and quickly ducked into the girls' bathroom. Andy stood outside the door for two minutes after the bell rang and then gave up in despair. Now he had no doubt at all. Melissa was definitely avoiding him.

Determined to confront her, he waited for her after school, but though he waited until the building was empty, he didn't see Melissa. Finally, he realized that she must have gone around the back side. He would have to go to her house again. This time he didn't call; he walked straight over there.

When Mrs. Gaylord opened the door, he said, "Tell Melissa I want to see her right away."

Mrs. Gaylord said apologetically, "I'm sorry, Melissa can't come out right now. She's busy getting ready for the dance. Can she call you later?"

"Tell Melissa if she doesn't come out on the porch and talk to me, I'm not going to the dance," Andy said.

"Very well, Andy," Mrs. Gaylord said. She appeared somewhat flustered by Andy's firmness.

Melissa arrived about four minutes later. "Did you want to see me, Andy?"

"You know I wanted to see you," Andy said. "It's about the costume. I'm not going to wear that costume."

"Oh, Andy. You're so silly. Why are you getting so upset about a silly thing like a costume?"

"I'm not upset," Andy replied. "I'm just not wearing it."

Melissa's smile faded. "Listen Andy, I've put up with enough from you. You promised you'd go to the dance with me, and anyone who goes to the dance with me has to wear that costume and that's that."

"Then get another date," Andy said. "I'm not wearing a Romeo costume."

Tears of rage sprang to Melissa's eyes. "You are just the meanest person in the whole world, Andy Johnson. You are just horrible! After I've told everyone in the whole school that we're going to the dance together, you're going to dump me! Where am I going to get a date on this late notice?"

"It wouldn't be this late if you'd talked to me earlier," Andy pointed out. He put his hand on Melissa's shoulder and said, "Don't cry, Melissa. Please don't cry."

Melissa's expression brightened immediately. Leaning her head on his shoulder and looking up at him with her bright blue eyes, she asked in a wavering voice, "Then you will go to the dance with me, Andy? Remember you promised."

Andy's feet suddenly seemed to weigh a thousand pounds. She was right. He had. He couldn't just walk off now. It just didn't fit his image of himself. He'd never thought of himself as the sort of person who broke his word. Finally, he said, "Melissa, I'll take you to the dance."

"And you'll wear the Romeo costume?" Melissa asked.

"But it's the last time."

Melissa laughed. "Silly! Halloween only comes once a year."

"No. I mean it's the last time I'm taking you out," Andy said.

"Oh, I doubt that," Melissa said, suddenly sure of herself.

"You don't understand . . . I haven't

been honest with you. It's Lori. . . . It's always been Lori."

"Oh, I know that," Melissa replied. "Everyone knows that. But Lori's not right for you, you know."

Andy was astonished. How had she known? Why wasn't she crushed? All this time he had been dreading a scene, thinking that Melissa would be heartbroken, or at the very least upset, and she was taking it all so calmly. Didn't she believe him? Did she know something that he didn't know? Was it that Lori was not interested in him? That she had another boyfriend? His head was spinning.

"All I care about right now," Melissa continued, "is that you keep your word." Her voice was cold. "You can't back out now, Andy. I've told all the kids that we're going to the party as Romeo and Juliet. I'll expect you here at seven-thirty."

"All right, Melissa," Andy said. "But this is the last time." How could he ever have found Melissa appealing? Or pretty? But that didn't matter now. He was free. Free to find Lori again.

* * *

Lori went to the Halloween dance alone. Though both Joe and Bud had asked her, she decided to express her re-found independence. Her reasoning was simple enough; if she went with a date, she'd be stuck with him all evening. If she went alone, she could be a free agent, and she might get a chance to talk to Andy. Though they were now back on speaking terms, every time she'd seen him he'd been with a lot of people. She'd thought about calling him on the telephone but hadn't had the nerve. The more she thought about their last argument, the clearer she saw his side of it. She now was willing to concede that he had a point. Her period of whirlwind dating had been unsatisfactory to her, and she was never going to be carried away with that nonsense again. Sure, she'd date if she wanted to, but she wasn't going to try to make herself a popularity queen. She was going to be herself. That would have to be good enough for any boy she dated.

As she got ready to go to the dance, she rehearsed the speech she would make to Andy if she could get to talk to him alone. Melissa had been out of school most of the week, and Andy had seemed very absentminded and busy. She supposed that he was worried about Melissa. Now that Melissa was back in school, they would probably be all wrapped up in each other. Maybe she wouldn't get a chance to talk to Andy tonight, but she would make him listen to her very soon. There was no reason to let her best friend go without a struggle.

Lori liked her Halloween costume. She looked at her bare feet, her short cut-off jeans, the bright red suspenders, and the checked man's shirt with the rolled-up sleeves and nodded her approval to the reflection in the mirror.

Her mother drove her to the dance, and Lori assured her that she could get a ride home with one of the other girls who would be there stag. At first it felt funny to walk in solo, while the other kids were entering the room in pairs or groups of three, four, or five. She felt vulnerable and unprotected like those heroines in romantic novels. Then she laughed at the thought of herself as unprotected. Who did she need to be protected from? She knew everyone in the room.

The first person she saw was Sally Gardner, who called out to her, "Oh, Lori, are you alone?" And when Lori replied yes, Sally asked, "Could you take Charleen's place at the punch bowl? She got a date at the last minute, and now we don't have anyone to help us."

Lori agreed to help serve punch. It was something to do besides stand around and feel awkward. She actually had a good time pouring as people paid their twenty-five cents. The music was fun, and she got to see everyone's costume. It was a good dance with a rock band that was just loud enough. The band members were all in black leotards and black tee shirts. Their faces were painted orange with heavy black marks made to look like cut-out pumpkins. Although it was a band that was often hired for Orleans High School dances, their music sounded especially good.

Lori passed the first hour and a half

of the dance saying hello to all of her friends who came by, pouring punch, and collecting money. When Melissa and Andy walked into the room wearing their Romeo and Juliet outfits, Lori cheerfully waved hello to them. Melissa did not wave back, but Andy did. He looked ill at ease in his scarlet tights and fingered the bent cardboard sword hanging from his belt. Melissa seemed to be having a good time. She was laughing and chattering gaily.

At eleven-thirty the costume parade began. Everyone lined up and walked around in a large circle. The art teacher and two Cape Cod landscape artists were the judges. Lori, knowing that her Huck Finn costume had absolutely no chance of winning a prize, begged out of the contest. Since she was performing a necessary function at the punch bowl, she was allowed to slip into the background.

She watched Andy and Melissa arguing. Lori could see that it must be about whether or not they would get in the parade. She watched Andy's face redden with anger. Melissa grabbed his hand and pulled him into the line.

Holding her chin high, she more or less dragged Andy round and round the circle.

Lori stood with her hands in the pockets of her cut-off jeans and admired Melissa's soft golden curls. No wonder Andy was crazy about her. No wonder he allowed her to make such a fool of him. She was surprised when Andy and Melissa were given third prize for costumes. If she had been a judge, she wouldn't have given Andy any prize at all. He looked too uncomfortable to be a prize winner.

If Melissa was happy about being in the contest, she seemed to be even happier about the prize. She accepted the large orange pumpkin, which was sporting a derby hat with the pink third-class ribbon on the side, as though it were a crown of gold. Melissa turned and said to Andy, "You see. I told you you looked good tonight."

They were standing close enough for Lori to hear Andy's reply. It was, "Do you want me to put the pumpkin in the car?"

Melissa nodded yes as though she were dismissing a servant. She turned to call to Pat, who was across the room.

"Oh Pat, you haven't danced with me this evening." She left Andy standing holding the pumpkin and ran over to where Pat was standing with a group of boys.

Pat looked pleasantly surprised as Melissa led him out on the dance floor.

Lori, figuring that this was a good opportunity, stepped out from behind the counter. "You watch the punch bowl for a while. I want to dance with Andy," she explained to Sally. She walked over to where Andy was standing clutching the prize pumpkin.

"What about dancing with me instead of that pumpkin?" she asked.

Startled, Andy turned around. His eyes lit up. "First, let's get rid of this thing," he said.

"I'll walk you to the car," Lori offered.

He looked down at her bare feet. "You can't go out like that. Why don't you wait here for me? I'll be right back."

Lori saw a light drift of snow floating down over the cool late fall landscape. Hugging her arms around her chest, she said, "I'll wait right here. This is the coldest fall I ever remember."

Andy ran out of the gym and down the steps, disappearing into the black night. He was back in two minutes, his cheeks bright red, breathing frost from the cold night air.

The band was taking a break, and the school committee was playing a soft, slow record. Lori said, "We don't have to dance. We can just talk."

"I can dance to this," Andy said quickly.

Lori looked at him in some surprise and asked, "Really? How did you learn?" Melissa must have taught him. She was sorry she'd asked and continued quickly, "Well, maybe you can dance to it, but I'm not sure I can. Promise me if I step on your toes too much, we'll quit."

"I promise," Andy said and held out his arms to her.

Lori let Andy put one hand on her waist to guide her through the crowd. They stepped out onto the dance floor and Lori stumbled. Then she realized that she was supposed to walk backwards. She was moving perfectly well by the time they had circled the floor once.

Andy said, "I knew you could do it."

"I wanted to talk to you," Lori began.

"That's why I asked you to dance. I wanted to apologize."

"You don't have to apologize," Andy said. "I've been crazy lately."

"So have I," Lori admitted. "I don't even understand why we've been fighting so much lately, but I do miss you, Andy. I miss you a lot. And you were right about being silly. I was silly. But I'm not silly anymore. I came to the dance alone."

Andy raised one eyebrow and asked, "Alone? I thought you had twenty-five boyfriends."

Lori laughed. "Not twenty-five, but I did have a couple of invitations. I decided that I would have a better time alone."

"You're a funny girl, Lori," Andy said. "Most girls hate to come to dances alone."

Lori wondered what Andy meant when he called her a funny girl. Did he want her to be like Melissa? Well, she didn't care what it meant. She was going to be herself.

She took a deep breath and tried again. "I've been doing a lot of thinking about us, Andy, and I want to be good friends again. I don't want to let your romance with Melissa interfere, and I don't want to let my dates interfere. The most important thing to me is your friendship, and I want to be your friend again." Breathlessly she waited for Andy's reply.

"Listen Lori," Andy began. "We can't just be *friends*—"

Lori felt tears gather behind her eyelids. She tried again. "I know I've been acting funny lately, Andy, and I'm sorry. I promise you we'll go back to the good old days. Everything will be just the way it was. You'll see."

"Things will never be the same between us," Andy said. He squeezed her hand. For the first time, she was aware of the pressure of his hand on her waist. It felt good to have Andy touching her. And when he increased his pressure to get her to turn, she felt a thrill run up and down her spine. She didn't have time to think about her reaction because Melissa's high, thin voice called, "Oh, Andy, come over here."

Andy said, "I have to finish talking to you tomorrow, Lori. I'll be able to explain it to you then."

Lori nodded, fighting back the tears

that threatened to spill out over her eyes. Pulling her hand away from Andy's, she walked back to the punch bowl. In frozen sadness, she watched Andy join Melissa and they disappeared into the crowd.

12

Lori was up at six-thirty the next morning. Her dreams had been troubled, and she'd slept intermittently. When the sky got light, she got up.

Pulling on her jogging suit, she decided to take a run down to the park and back. Lori ran for the first few blocks as though she were an old lady, but she soon limbered up. She picked up speed and ran as fast as she could. The physical exercise, the working up a sweat, felt good to her, and she was glad she'd decided to get out and do something rather than stay at home and worry. Andy was a good sleeper, and since he'd obviously been out late the night before, he wouldn't call her until at least noon.

This gave her a sense of freedom—of living on borrowed time. Whatever

Andy had to say, it would be unpleasant. She knew that. They'd had too
much trouble lately for it to be anything
else. Well, she would be ready for him
when he called. She would be tough
and strong and independent and free. If
he gave her a hard time, she'd tell him
that she didn't need him for a friend
anymore. She didn't need anyone.

As she raced into the wind with the
cold morning air biting her skin, she
was able to erase some of the bitterness
and disappointment she had felt about
her attempted conversation with Andy
last night. Maybe she wasn't the only
one who was changing. Maybe Andy
was changing, too.

She galloped along the streets, past
the seacoast and bays and down to the
shopping center. Then she turned
around and ran back. When she got
home, it was ten o'clock in the morning, and she felt pretty good. Whatever
Andy wanted to say to her, she would be
able to handle.

She walked into the house and found
a note on the kitchen table, which read,
"Gone grocery shopping. Andy says
meet him at Orleans Wharf at noon."

Lori walked upstairs, stripped off her

running suit, went into the bathroom, washed her dark brown hair, and scrubbed all over. She felt as though the act of cleansing her body was somehow connected with the cleansing of her spirits. She rubbed herself briskly, holding her long, strong arms up in the air and letting the water play on her back as she scrubbed with the back brush. Finally, she stepped out of the shower, towel-dried her hair and body, slipped on her bright pink robe, and went into her room to dress.

By the time she was dressed, it was after eleven. Lori decided to walk down to the pier rather than take the bus. Since her mother was still gone, there was no hope of borrowing the family car. She thought of calling Andy and asking him to pick her up. His car was always available, but she decided against it. Andy and she weren't that kind of friends anymore. If he had to make a formal appointment to see her, so be it. Whatever was coming, she could handle.

The walk down to the Orleans pier was a slower repeat of her run that morning. This time she had a chance to enjoy the dark green pine trees that grew along the suburban Cape Cod houses. The sun was out, and it was a lovely day. Crisp and cool. There was no sign of the snow that had fallen the night before, and many of the yards were speckled with orange-and-gold leaves.

Lori enjoyed the walk, pacing herself so that she arrived at the edge of the Orleans Wharf at ten minutes of twelve. To her surprise, Andy was already there, sitting on a bench, staring out at the open blue sea. He was holding flowers in his hand, a small bouquet of white carnations and a few deep red berry-like plants that had small red blossoms on them. They were wrapped in green tissue paper.

Andy held out the flowers to her. "They're for you," he said hoarsely.

Lori couldn't believe it. Was it some kind of joke? Had Andy bought her flowers to say good-bye? She took the flowers, reaching up to touch the small red blossoms. "No one's ever bought me flowers—ever," she whispered.

"Well, I did," Andy said, "and I've got to tell you why."

Their voices were hushed. Lori realized that she was close to tears. Darn it, she thought, I promised myself I wouldn't do this. Tearing her gaze away from the flowers, she looked out at the ocean and said, "I still think we could be friends if we tried."

Andy shook his head and he, too, seemed to be staring at some far distant point on the horizon of the sea. "We'll never be *friends* again, Lori, no matter what we do. You see, the problem is . . ." and his voice broke as he faltered. "The problem is, I love you, Lori. I've loved you for a long time."

The blood drained from Lori's face, but she tried to keep her voice light. "Would you run through that one more time, please?"

Andy turned to face her. His bright blue eyes were sparkling with an agonized intensity as he said in a fast, desperate voice, "I can't help it, Lori. I honestly can't help it. I just can't get over it. I know you're not interested in me, but that's the way it is."

"But what about Melissa?"

"She's through with me," Andy said.

Lori's heart lurched. So that was the problem! Andy had just come to her for comfort. "Andy, I know you're disappointed about Melissa. I don't blame you. But you'll find someone else—"

"Lori! You're not listening! You don't understand! It's never been Melissa! It's you I'm in love with! Why can't you understand that?"

He sounded so frantic that Lori instinctively reached out and put her hand on his shoulder. "Andy," she said, "I'm not sure what this is all about, but I hate to see you so upset. I want you to be happy, honestly I do, but are you sure—?"

Andy's voice rose. "Lori!" he shouted. I AM NOT IN LOVE WITH MELISSA! I NEVER HAVE BEEN! The whole thing was a trick to try to keep you! I couldn't think of any other way—" his voice trailed off.

"A trick?" Lori repeated dumbly. "A trick? Where did you think I was going?"

"Well, you were dating all those guys, and you wouldn't go out with me—"

"Those guys mean nothing to me," Lori said. "I don't know why I even went out with them. Maybe I was jealous of Melissa."

"I can't imagine a girl like you being jealous of Melissa," Andy said.

"A girl like me? I wonder what kind of girl I really am?"

"Well, I was beginning to wonder, too," Andy said, "what with you making up to Sammy like that and kissing Joe—"

"Kissing Joe!" Lori said indignantly. "If you only knew how awful that was!" She made a face and added, "I've pretty much decided that I'm not the romantic type. I let two or three guys kiss me, and it wasn't all that great."

"Seems like you had the wrong partner," Andy said, his eyes twinkling. He drew Lori to him and kissed her firmly on the mouth.

Her lips curved happily beneath his sweet, warm pressure. Should she admit to him that he was absolutely, one hundred percent right?

6 brand new Silhouette Romance novels yours for 15 days–Free!

If you enjoyed this Silhouette First Love, and would like to move on to even more thrilling, satisfying stories then Silhouette Romances are for you. Enjoy the challenges, conflicts, and joys of love. Sensitive heroines will enchant you—powerful heroes will delight you as they sweep you off to adventures around the world.

6 Silhouette Romances, free for 15 days!

We'll send you 6 new Silhouette Romances to keep for 15 days, absolutely free! If you decide not to keep them, send them back to us. You pay nothing.

FREE HOME DELIVERY. But if you enjoy them as much as we think you will, keep them by paying the invoice enclosed with your free trial shipment. You'll then automatically become a member of the Silhouette Book Club and receive 6 more new Silhouette Romances every month.

There is no minimum number of books to buy and you can cancel at any time.

— — — — — This offer expires May 31, 1983 — — — — —

 Silhouette Book Club, Dept. SF0272
120 Brighton Road, Clifton, NJ 07012

Please send me 6 Silhouette Romances to keep for 15 days, absolutely free. I understand I am not obligated to join the Silhouette Book Club unless I decide to keep them.

NAME _____

ADDRESS _____

CITY _____

STATE _____ ZIP _____

First Love from Silhouette

Look for These
New First Love Romances from
Silhouette Books Next Month

Dare To Love

Nancy Bush

When life seemed to be passing her by,
mild mannered Abby decided it was time
for a drastic change. The result surprised
everyone, and most especially dark eyed
David who certainly had never expected
to meet SUPERWOMAN.

The First Act

Anne London

Gerry's starring role in the school play gave
her a chance at fame and fortune. And when
her friend, Aristo, champion goalie of the
hockey team, encouraged her to take a long
shot, she knew she just had to try it.

First Love from Silhouette

THERE'S NOTHING QUITE AS SPECIAL AS A __FIRST LOVE.__

$1.75 each

1 ☐ NEW BOY IN TOWN
Francis

2 ☐ GIRL IN THE ROUGH
Wunsch

3 ☐ PLEASE LET ME IN
Beckman

4 ☐ SERENADE
Marceau

5 ☐ FLOWERS FOR LISA
Ladd

6 ☐ KATE HERSELF
Erskine

7 ☐ SONGBIRD
Enfield

10 ☐ PLEASE LOVE ME
. . . SOMEBODY
Johnson

11 ☐ IT'S MY TURN
Carr

12 ☐ IN MY SISTER'S
SHADOW
Dellin

13 ☐ SOMETIME MY
LOVE
Ryan

14 ☐ PROMISED KISS
Ladd

15 ☐ SUMMER ROMANCE
Diamond

16 ☐ SOMEONE TO LOVE
Bryan

17 ☐ GOLDEN GIRL
Erskine

18 ☐ WE BELONG
TOGETHER
Harper

19 ☐ TOMORROW'S WISH
Ryan

20 ☐ SAY PLEASE!
Francis

21 ☐ TEACH ME TO LOVE
Davis

22 ☐ THAT SPECIAL
SUMMER
Kent

$1.95 each

☐ WHEN SEPTEMBER
RETURNS
Jones

☐ DREAM LOVER
Treadwell

☐ THE PERSONAL TOUCH
Cooney

26 ☐ A TIME FOR US
Ryan

27 ☐ A SECRET PLACE
Francis

28 ☐ LESSON IN LOVE
West

29 ☐ FOR THE LOVE
OF LORI
Ladd

30 ☐ A BOY TO DREAM
ABOUT
Quinn

FIRST LOVE, Department FL/4
1230 Avenue of the Americas
New York, NY 10020

Please send me the books I have checked above. I am
enclosing $_____ (please add 50¢ to cover postage
and handling. NYS and NYC residents please add ap-
propriate sales tax). Send check or money order—no
cash or C.O.D.'s please. Allow six weeks for delivery.

NAME_____

ADDRESS_____

CITY_____STATE/ZIP_____

READERS' COMMENTS ON FIRST LOVE BOOKS

"I am very pleased with the First Love Books by Silhouette. Thank you for making a book that I can enjoy."

—G.O.*, Indianapolis, IN

"I just want you to know that I love the Silhouette First Love Books. They put me in a happy mood. Please don't stop selling them!"

—M.H.*, Victorville, CA

"I loved the First Love book that I read. It was great! I loved every single page of it. I plan to read many more of them."

—R.B.*, Picayune, MS

*names available upon request